A COLD
DARK
PROMISE

A COLD
DARK
PROMISE

Toni Anderson

A Cold Dark Promise
Copyright © 2017 Toni Anderson
Cover design by Regina Wamba of ReginaWamba.com

For more information on Toni Anderson's books, sign up for her newsletter, or check out her website (www.toniandersonauthor.com).

ALSO BY TONI ANDERSON

For Aimee.

CHAPTER ONE

S UNSHINE SHOWCASED THE cherry blossoms that lined the Tidal Basin, and glinted off the white marble of the Jefferson Memorial in an almost blinding light. Alex Parker maneuvered his Audi carefully through beltway commuter traffic, as he and his fiancée, FBI Agent Mallory Rooney, headed into the heart of the nation's capital. They drove downtown, the smell of exhaust fumes mingling with the scents wafting from the multitudes of food trucks that lined the streets. Tourists bustled. Buses full of schoolchildren headed in the direction of the Capitol Building.

He and Mal had rented a condo in Quantico for those nights they worked late and didn't want to drive back to his DC apartment. Their new house should be ready to move into in a few weeks' time, after they returned from their honeymoon.

"I'm getting fat." Mallory smoothed two hands over her rounded stomach. She was twenty-seven weeks pregnant and looked more beautiful with each passing day. That was pretty much how long he'd known this woman who'd changed his life from darkness to light.

"I think that's how it's supposed to work," he said gently. Her hair had grown a little longer than when they'd first met. It now formed a dark cap with the ends just starting to curl

1

around that elfin face. They were getting married a week from Saturday.

"I'm not sure this reproduction business is divided equally between the sexes," she said dryly.

"Hey, I did my part."

"Your part involved a few minutes of vigorous exercise." She sounded particularly unimpressed. He'd have to fix that later.

"I recall going above and beyond the call of duty." He gave her a salacious grin.

Amber eyes promised vengeance, even as a small smile flirted with her mouth. "Do you now," she said slowly.

He squeezed her fingers. "I promise to make it up to you after the baby is born."

Mallory's eyes softened. "I know you will."

He let go of her hand to change gear.

"I'm going to look like the side of a barn in our wedding photos," she mused.

"You can barely tell you're pregnant." He loved every expanding inch of her.

She stared distractedly at her bump. "I'll have to get the seamstress to leave extra room for everything I eat this week. Or starve myself."

"Hell, no," he said sharply. "We can get married naked for all I care, but you are not going to starve yourself to fit into some stupid dress."

One side of her lips quirked. "My dress is a work of art."

"*You* are the work of art."

"And *that* is why I love you." Her hands kept up a steady soothing motion over her abdomen. "I don't think the minister would approve of us turning up naked, but it might

2

be worth it to see the look on everyone's faces."

"Give me the word."

Mallory smiled, and his heart rate settled a little. The idea of her not taking care of herself, or getting stressed, scared the hell out of him. On New Year's Eve, they'd thought she'd lost the baby. Then, in February, he'd believed for a few horrifying minutes she'd been murdered in her hotel room. They'd been the worst moments of his life, which, as a former assassin who'd spent months incarcerated in a Moroccan jail, was saying something.

"We could always elope to Vegas," he suggested.

"You wish."

She was right. She knew him too well.

She grew serious. "I'm sorry I forced you into this rigmarole. I know you'd rather skip all the drama." There was that twist in his heart again. "It's just that Mom and Dad..." she trailed off.

Mallory's twin sister, Payton, had been abducted when they were both eight years old. The family had finally discovered what had happened to Mal's twin and had laid her to rest last December.

"The payoff is worth the price," he assured her.

She smiled, but guilt lingered in her eyes.

"I *really* don't mind the wedding stuff." He had to remind himself to not call it "crap" whenever he spoke to Mal. "I just don't want you stressing about things like how you look or what you wear. You're beautiful. You being pregnant with our baby is the sexiest damn thing I have ever seen. Every time I look at you I fall in love all over again. Your health and the baby's are the only things that concern me. Turn up in rags and I'll marry you. Hell, turn up painted green and I won't

3

blink."

"I like that idea."

"Nontoxic paint," he cautioned.

"Yes, dear."

He grinned. They pulled up outside *Blissed*, a fancy bridal store with more tulle in the window than the Bolshoi ballet. He got out of the car and walked around to open her door.

"You're going to pick up the tuxes, right?" she asked, gathering her bag and taking his arm so he could help ease her up and out of his low-slung sports car. Most days, Mallory wore a business suit to work. Today, she was wearing a white, cotton sundress printed with yellow daises and a gauzy, white cardigan that made him think of long, hot summers and picnics in cornfields. Her sidearm was in her purse.

"Yes, ma'am. Frazer is picking up his own. I'm picking up the others." Assistant Special Agent in Charge Lincoln Frazer—Mallory's boss—was Alex's best man. His groomsmen included FBI agent Lucas Randall and two former Army buddies he'd reconnected with after years of silence.

Dermot Gray and Haley Cramer, his business partners, rounded out his side of the wedding party. "I'm going into the office to check in with Haley and Dermot and the guys on the cybercrimes team." Everyone who worked for him was invited to the wedding. That meant they were setting up an emergency room in the hotel to run any ongoing operations and to be available in case of any new intrusions. A few of them would need to remain sober but no one would miss the party completely. "Pick you up in an hour?"

She shook her head. "Mom invited us to lunch."

The muscles in his chest tightened.

"I told her you were busy so you can thank me later. I'll get a cab back to the apartment when we're done."

He kissed her forehead. "And that is one of the many reasons I love you."

She smoothed her palm over his cheek. "One of the reasons."

They stood on the sidewalk not going anywhere for several long minutes. He never got tired of kissing her.

She pulled away, looking as dazed as he felt. "Is Haley picking up her dress or should I get it delivered with the others?"

"I'll ask her."

Mallory eyed him knowingly. "Is she still pissed she isn't your best man?"

Alex took her hand and pressed her fingers to his lips. "She'll get over it."

"Eventually." Mal already knew his business partner well enough to realize Haley would make him suffer long and hard before she forgave him.

"I invited her to my hen weekend," Mal said suddenly.

Alex felt the blood drain from his head. "Did she say yes?"

"She hasn't replied yet."

Haley and Dermot had been his best friends at MIT. Of the three of them, Haley was the free-spirited wild child. She came from money and had fronted the startup costs for their company. She was razor sharp and partied like the world might end tomorrow. He loved her like a sister, but god help the man who fell *in* love with her.

"If she gets you into trouble, I'm going to kidnap her and dump her on her Caribbean island for a month. Alone. I might make it two months and arrange a food drop."

"Then she really will kill you."

"She'll have to catch me first." He sighed. "I need to find her a decent boyfriend."

Mallory punched his arm. "You don't need to find her anything. She's more than capable of finding her own man."

Alex shook his head. "She's attracted to douchebags. I'm going to try and find her a nice guy who doesn't mind a few sharp edges."

Mallory smoothed her hand down the front of his shirt, her engagement ring shimmering like a small sun in the morning light. "She'll find someone. The worst thing you can do is try to set her up."

Alex's mouth quirked. "Maybe she'll meet someone at the wedding."

His only jobs for the big day, aside from turning up, were figuring out the seating arrangements for the reception, and writing two-hundred or so name place cards as per the wedding planner's orders. Apparently, first-come, first-served, didn't fly in these social circles. Considering how many politicians were on the guest list that was a damned shame. Maybe he'd surround Haley with every eligible bachelor he knew, but then she really might kill him. He'd wanted to hire someone to write the cards for him, or have them printed, but the wedding planner said the personal touch made everything more authentic.

How could a card telling you where you were sitting at dinner determine the *authenticity* of someone's wedding vows?

Whatever. He'd get the damn cards written this week.

He checked his watch and looked at the front door of the little shop full of white froth. "Want me to come in with you?"

"No, thank you. We don't need any bad luck."

He grinned and pulled her to him again, kissing the tip of her nose and feeling their child kick against his stomach. He looked down. "Someone's feisty."

Mal laughed and placed his hand against her abdomen. "Tell me about it. This kid of ours is either going to be a kick-boxer or a soccer player."

"You sure you're okay?" He searched her features for signs of fatigue, but her skin was soft and smooth as peaches and she practically glowed with happiness.

"I am perfect."

He swallowed the ache in his throat.

"I'll text you once I finish up with my mother. See you back at the apartment, and we can take Rex for a stroll together."

Rex was their golden retriever who'd been rescued after his owner was brutally murdered. He stayed with Alex's neighbor whenever they were away overnight, just until they got into their new home. Fortunately, Rex was used to apartment living.

"Sounds like a plan." Alex watched Mallory walk away, wondering how he'd ever gotten this lucky.

An hour later, he parked outside the brownstone in Woodley Park that housed Cramer, Parker & Gray, Security Consultants. Five carefully packaged, custom-tailored tuxes were stacked in the trunk. Haley's gown was being delivered with the bridesmaids' dresses. His cell phone pinged with a message from an unknown user as he headed up the steps. He stopped and read the text.

He stood for a moment and contemplated ignoring the summons. Then he closed his eyes and swore. Pivoting on his heel, he strode north-west along Connecticut Avenue. At least it was warm out. Scenting coffee, he found a nearby Starbucks and grabbed two cups of dark roast. He crossed the street and entered the National Zoo, mingling with tourists and parents pushing strollers around the large enclosures. A tingle of excitement shot through him. This could be him soon, showing his child the joys of animals and the natural world.

Alex meandered through the crowd, making sure he wasn't followed. After circuiting the entire zoo, he doubled back to the panda enclosure—the zoo's pride and joy—and found a vacant bench. He placed the second coffee on a wooden strut and rested his arm along the back of the seat. The big, male panda was out of his den and walking laps around his compound, examining the walls as if looking for an escape.

Sudden panic scratched at the edges of Alex's mind like sharp claws on a dirt wall. Memories of being imprisoned hit him—filth, pain, despair. He forced himself to breathe slowly and steadily. He wasn't in that Moroccan shit hole anymore. He wasn't at someone else's mercy.

The bench seat creaked as someone sat next to him. Alex held out the second cup of coffee he'd bought, and the woman took it from him gingerly, careful not to touch his skin.

She'd skipped the power suit this morning and had gone with workout gear—black yoga pants with a black zippered hoodie fastened to her chin. Bright orange Nikes provided the only splash of color, and she wore a neat leather bag strapped around her waist. Maybe she thought she might need to run from him. Not a good sign.

"Jane." He nodded carefully.

Once upon a time, he'd despised Jane Sanders, who'd acted as a go-between for the heads of The Gateway Project and its foot soldiers. Now he pitied her.

Unease was visible in the wideness of her eyes and the tension that emanated from her frame. She scraped her white-blonde hair behind one ear. Her hand shook.

She was terrified of him. She had always been terrified of him. So why seek him out now?

"Mr. Parker." Her voice was rough.

Alex raised his brows. "I thought you'd started to call me Alex?"

Her lips pinched, and she looked away, staring into the distance, not seeing the panda or the crowds.

"I found my daughter," she said slowly.

Everything in the world muted.

Four years ago, Jane Sanders had obeyed a court order to let her four-year-old daughter visit her father for the summer. Jane had never seen the child again. An international arrest warrant had been issued, but her ex had disappeared.

Her fingers played with the hem of her jacket, knuckles prominent and white against soft, pink skin. "Ahmed is on a yacht in the south of France. Antibes. Taylor is with him."

"How do you know?"

"A friend of mine spotted him."

"Then Masook is already gone." Ahmed Masook was a wealthy man who wouldn't take chances with his liberty.

Jane swallowed. She had sharp, delicate features. A short, straight nose and vivid, blue eyes and chalk-white skin that would burn rather than tan. "He didn't see my friends. He doesn't know them. He's still there. They both are."

"So, go to the authorities," Alex said impatiently. He wasn't her stooge. He didn't have time for this. He was getting married next week. They weren't friends. They'd never been friends.

"He must have paid the cops off. He wouldn't be there otherwise. If I go to them he'll know. He'll run."

Alex rolled his shoulders and leaned forward so his forearms rested on his knees, still cradling his paper cup of coffee. Birds sang in the trees that bristled with new leaves. Daffodils nodded their yellow heads in time with the wind.

"Help me grab Taylor, and get us back to the US. I'll take care of things from there."

"You're asking me to take a child away from her father," he said calmly.

"He stole her from me!" Her eyes burned electric blue. She put the coffee cup down, untasted, hands gripping one another like tangled vines. "I was willing to abide by the court order. I was willing to share Taylor for all our sakes. But Masook didn't want that. He didn't like the fact I left him and took our daughter. He thinks he's above the law."

Now that Alex was going to be a father, he'd gained a better understanding of Jane's anguish. And Masook's.

Jane grabbed his hand. "I'm *begging* you."

The fact that she touched him was astonishing. She'd always been petrified of him. Yet she'd come to him for help.

Her eyes sprang wide as she realized what she'd done. She released him and inched farther away. Then her lower jaw thrust out mutinously and her eyes narrowed. "I could threaten you and your precious fiancée. I could rip your world apart."

Alex held her gaze as everything inside him stilled. A little piece of his soul tore loose and drifted away on the breeze.

"I could. But I won't." Her expression turned stricken. She stuffed her fists under her armpits as if deathly cold. "I'm just saying I could."

And he'd destroy her. But he didn't want to destroy her. She was already broken.

"Taylor might not even remember you anymore."

Her mouth warped as her expression shattered. "I know. But I also know the kind of man Ahmed is." Her fists clenched and unclenched in her lap. "I will not abandon my baby to that monster." She started to sob.

Alex didn't want to be moved by her impassioned plea. He stared at his shoes. Jane was young. She could have more children. Even as he thought it he knew it wouldn't matter. One child did not replace another.

She stood, wiping her cheeks. "What would you do, if it was your child?"

Alex had the knowledge and skills to go after anyone who threatened his family, which was why Jane had come to him. He'd tear the world apart inch-by-inch until he found them. But he wasn't a killer for hire, or someone's pet mercenary.

Jane seemed to understand his decision without him saying a word. She closed her eyes and appeared to sway in the gentle breeze.

"What are you going to do?" He couldn't get involved. He was getting married in a week's time. He had no authority in France. He didn't even like Jane Sanders.

But he understood her.

Her chin lifted. "I'll go myself."

"You'll die or get arrested."

The grief in her eyes was haunting and familiar. "I'd rather die than never get my little girl back."

Alex thought of his own mother's gentle touch. Her loving smile. Her warm hugs. He imagined Mallory in Jane's place. It didn't matter. He knew what his answer had to be. He couldn't help Jane.

Silently, she stood and walked away.

CHAPTER TWO

M ALLORY OPENED HER small suitcase and began tossing things in for her bachelorette weekend. Rather than go to a bar—she was pregnant after all—she'd organized a relaxing couple of days at a spa in Virginia, not far from the vineyard where she and Alex planned to tie the knot a week from Saturday.

In reality, the knot had been tied months ago. Alex was hers. She was his. They'd made their vows in that snowy woods, deep in the heart of West Virginia, with a serial killer bearing witness. But perhaps it was as important to do it in the light, before friends and family and not surrounded by the taint of evil.

She wanted them to be a family. Happy. United. In every way possible. She wanted him to know the depth of her feelings, of her commitment, to both him and their child.

She shot him a glance, wondering if he was at all nervous. He lay on the bed, staring at the ceiling. He was naked, and they'd devoted the last hour to making love. Not a bad way to spend her day off.

She found a bathing suit that would hopefully stretch over her ever-expanding bump and tossed it in the case, along with a novel she'd been wanting to read. In all honesty, she'd rather stay home with Alex, but her mom was excited and determined to milk the mother-of-the-bride experience for everything it was worth. As this would be her only chance, Mallory was indulging her.

Mallory touched the curve of her stomach, the fluttering movement from within reassuring her anxious heart. Margret Tremont understood how committed she and Alex were to one another. How *unbreakable* their bond. But maybe that's how her mother had felt about her father before their lives had been ripped apart by her sister's abduction.

Almost losing this baby had been terrifying. Taking things for granted was foolish, especially in her line of work and with Alex's past history. Mallory was trying to learn to enjoy each moment—beginning with relaxing and having fun this weekend. Getting pampered and stealing some much-needed sleep.

Besides, it had been a long time since she'd simply hung out with girlfriends. A long, long time. As much as she loved Alex, she needed her friends, too. Their child would need friends, playmates, siblings. They'd need their community.

Her bridesmaids were her two best friends from college and FBI Agent Ashley Chen, who she'd bonded with since they'd started working together a few months ago. Ashley was dating one of Mallory's oldest friends, Lucas Randall, who was also a groomsman, so it made sense to include her in the wedding party. The main issue was figuring out where Ashley could conceal her weapon, as FBI agents were never officially off-duty. Mallory wasn't even going to try to wear her Glock. There would be more armed guests at this wedding than at most police academy graduations. She should be safe enough to take the day off.

She and Alex were going to split their time between this

apartment, which Alex was keeping because his firm was based in the city, and a beautiful old Victorian they'd found closer to the FBI Academy where they both spent most of their time working these days. Workmen had been renovating the Victorian for months, and Alex had been updating the security, but it should be ready for when they came back from their honeymoon in Hawaii.

Nothing but the beach and relaxation for two whole weeks. She couldn't wait.

She looked at Alex and realized something was wrong. She was naked and even when she wasn't, he spent most of his time watching her. Not in a creepy stalker way. But in an *I-can't-believe-I-got-this-lucky* kind of way. It had been distracting at first, and always flattering. Right now, he wasn't paying her any attention.

He was brooding.

Uh oh.

"What's up?" she asked him.

He glanced toward her and grimaced. He said nothing so she came closer and straddled his hips, settling her weight on his warm skin and lean muscle. She traced her hands over his stomach.

"I can make you tell me." She grinned. But shadows moved across his silver eyes, turning them pewter.

He trapped her hands. "Jane Sanders contacted me today. I met her at the zoo."

"Oh." *Jane Sanders?* Mal went to move off him, but Alex gripped her thighs.

"What do you know about her?" he asked.

Mal frowned. Jane Sanders bothered her for many reasons, chief amongst them was Jane had worked for her mother and

15

had been involved in The Gateway Project. Jane had left DC once Mal's mother had stepped down from the senate. Mal had assumed that would be the last they'd ever hear from the woman.

"Not much. What does she want? Is she going to cause trouble for us?" This was her one true fear. That someone would reveal Alex's past and she'd lose him. She could not lose him. He said he had safeguards in place. She trusted him, but she worried...

He rolled them so they faced each other on the bed, and touched her face. "It's okay. We're okay." He drew in a breath that spoke of regrets and misgivings. "Her ex-husband's a wealthy Saudi businessman who snatched their kid during his first visitation four years ago. Kid will be eight now."

Mallory's mouth opened in shock. Being pregnant had changed her perspective about a lot of things. Must be the hormones, but all her emotions seemed deeper now, more rounder, more fully formed.

"I didn't know. She never mentioned it." But why would anyone bring that up in casual conversation? Not to mention Mallory had been consumed by the mystery of what had happened to her own sister, consumed by her own pain.

"Why did she want to talk to you?" she asked.

"She got word the ex turned up on the French Riviera, and she wanted me to help snatch the kid back." He touched his forehead to hers. "I told her no. I'm getting married next week. I can't leave now."

"What did she say?" Mallory braced herself for threats and blackmail.

"That she'd do it herself."

Air deflated from her lungs and shame for being so caught

up in her own worries crept over her. It wasn't that long ago that she'd been the one desperate for answers.

They stopped talking. Alex's hand moved to cup her full breasts. He teased one nipple until she throbbed and moaned. She rolled onto her back as he explored her with strong hands and a clever mouth. She wanted to touch him, but he often seemed to need this—to touch and explore her like she was his magical place. He took his time, claiming every inch of skin as his own while her blood slowly heated.

Licks of pleasure spiraled into a cyclone of lust. His fingers dipped between her thighs and she moaned. Finding her ready, he turned her away from him, arranging a pillow beneath her baby bump and another cushioning her head. This was her favorite position now she was pregnant and he knew it. Alex moved behind her and slid deep inside and she came with a deep shudder. He leaned up, squeezed her nipple even as he thrust slowly in and out. She could lie like this for hours, days, it felt so good. She shook with pleasure, and she couldn't bear for it to change but...

"More, Alex. Deeper." It was a private joke between them, but the hoarseness of her voice took her by surprise. He got to her every single time.

He angled them slightly, and pressed deeper, touching that spot inside her that made her tremble and shudder and fly off that ledge again like a skydiver at terminal velocity. She cried out and he thrust faster, his hands gripping her hips as sweat made their bodies slick.

She ground against him and felt him stiffen as he came inside her. His fingers clinging to her like a man trying to save himself from drowning.

Their breathing quieted. Heartbeats slowed and melded.

The dying sun cast long shadows through their bedroom window.

"You have to help her," Mallory said quietly.

His arm curled over her hip, and he pulled her closer.

"I can take another week off work," she said.

"No way are you getting involved in this."

She looked over her shoulder and smiled. "You can't stop me."

He kissed her fingers and smiled sadly. "I know I can't stop you, but if you insist on coming with me, then I won't go."

His silver gaze wasn't angry or demanding. It was calm. Implacable. Mallory blew out a big breath of frustration. It was the first time Alex had refused to let her be involved in something. She knew he hid things from her occasionally. But the two of them had made a promise to one another the day investigators had uncovered her sister's body.

No more lies.

Ever.

And that was why he was telling her this now, she realized.

Her fingers gripped his, hugging him to her. "I don't want something bad to happen to you."

"I can take care of myself."

She swallowed. "I know you can, but I don't want you to have to take care of yourself. I want to look after you. I want to be the one watching your back."

He ran a finger down her spine and followed it with his lips.

She closed her eyes. "You know what I mean."

"I do. I feel it every time you go to work without me."

But he let her go anyway, because she needed the space to

do her job, and he respected that. He respected her.

She rolled onto her back. She didn't want Alex to go on this job without her, but she knew she wasn't the only one who needed space to work, even when that work wasn't clearly defined. She touched his face.

"I can't go." Alex insisted, but there was no conviction behind his words. "We have a wedding to prepare for and a dog to look after."

Rex was in the living room on the couch. He'd fetch a ball from dawn until dusk, but he was generally a couch potato which suited them both perfectly right now. Mallory intended to get a puppy or two after the wedding. She'd convince Alex by reminding him dogs were good security.

"All you have to do for the wedding is turn up—and write those place name cards. The wedding planner," who Alex had nicknamed the General for good reason, "is doing virtually everything else including arranging transportation for all the guests who are flying in. I can make any last-minute adjustments and double-check on the flowers and still go to work every day next week. Hiring that woman is the best idea you've ever had."

He laid his ear against her belly. "Not the *best* idea, but pretty inspired."

She sank her hands into his hair. "When will you be back?"

"I imagine Wednesday at the latest." He placed one large palm on her stomach and held her gaze. "I won't take any unnecessary risks, and I won't do anything stupid. If the child is there I will either figure out a way for the legat to get involved." The legat was the FBI's official presence in a foreign country. "Or I'll sneak them away when no one is looking and

19

bring her, and Jane, back to the States." Alex kissed her stomach again. She knew he was impatient to meet the newest member of their family. "I'm not sure the daughter—Taylor—will remember her mother after four years."

Mallory's heart clenched, and her hand went to where their baby was kicking her low ribs. Alex linked their fingers. She already felt overprotective. The idea of someone stealing her baby... She swallowed hard. This was important. Jane Sanders had always seemed a little aloof, and no wonder. Her child had been stolen and the fact it was by the father made it no less heartbreaking for the mother.

Mallory touched Alex's lips. "Don't be late for the wedding. Promise?"

Silver eyes met hers. "I promise."

CHAPTER THREE

T HE SUN WAS hot on the back of Alex's neck. It might only be April, but it was already in the nineties on the French Riviera. He wore sunglasses, white pants and a hand-tailored pastel pink shirt with the top two buttons undone. His cuffs were folded precisely, halfway up his forearms. His shoes were a tan leather. Italian. Expensive.

A brand-new SIG was strapped to his ankle. Ankle holsters were not his favorite place for concealed carry, but anyone wearing a jacket stood out in this heat, and he excelled at not standing out.

He, Jane, and Jack Reilly, one of the operatives from Cramer, Parker & Gray, had quickly overnighted it to Paris on the company's jet, then rented a small private plane to Nice. Alex's cover was that of a wealthy German national on holiday with his American wife. The American wife had been told to do nothing except wait patiently for his instruction. Something his real wife-to-be would have smacked him for suggesting. But if Ahmed Masook found out Jane was here, he'd run, and she'd never see her daughter again.

Alex would have left Jane in the States except the idea of being arrested on child abduction charges the week before his wedding was not his idea of fun. He had promises to keep, and he'd brought Jack Reilly along to help make that happen. He didn't completely trust Jane not to betray him in some way if it meant getting her child back.

Alex flicked through the news articles in the German newspaper, *Die Zeit,* while sipping a cappuccino. This particular coffee shop overlooked the marina in Port Vauban where the mere mortals moored their yachts. To his right was *Quai des Milliardaires* or Millionaires' Quay. Even the super-yachts had been superseded by the palatial mega-yachts, and if you had to ask the price of moorage you should probably just turn around and sail into the sunset.

Alex was loaded, but only Saudi princes and Russian oligarchs had that sort of money to burn.

Antibes was a beautiful town, rich with history and French artistry. The ocean was a deep azure blue so bright it made his eyes sting. Rows of brightly colored watercraft bobbed against the gray-green rock of the ancient harbor walls.

Thankfully the marina was busy—it made hiding in plain sight that much easier. A steady stream of people headed in and out of the harbor. Tourists explored the town behind him and the fort on the hill to the north. Locals drove by. Fishermen. Teens. Parents with small children. It was a beautiful setting, and he wished he was sharing it with Mal.

A woman with warm bronze skin and jewel-like, green eyes watched him from another table. He caught her stare. She blushed and looked away. She was beautiful but seemed out of place. Maybe because she was alone in a country where beautiful women were rarely alone for long. He finished his drink and signaled the waitress for the bill.

He spoke French with a strong German accent. "*Merci beaucoup.*" And left her a good tip.

Then he strolled past the small yachts of Port Vauban,

surveilling the area with a hidden camera attached to the top button of his shirt and another digital SLR hanging around his neck. A tourist with nothing to do but enjoy the day. He moved slowly, joked with a couple of men coming in off the water with sun-reddened cheeks, smiles, and a cooler full of fish.

Alex inhaled the smell of the Mediterranean, salt and water and the aroma of seaweed drying on the sunbaked rocks. After an hour or so he headed back past the cafe where the pretty woman still sat typing away on a laptop. He inclined his head when he caught her staring at him again. Then he adjusted his sunglasses, his fake wedding-band glinting in the sunshine.

Only one woman occupied his thoughts. Only one woman obsessed him. But maybe he was flattering himself. Maybe the beautiful, young lady was just enjoying the view. Or maybe she was the honey for some agencies' trap.

And, yes, he was cynical. A stint in a Moroccan jail and kill lists would do that to a man.

He started walking along the wide concrete expanse of the quay, toward the huge ocean-going palaces. It was quiet except for the occasional squawk of gulls and the chatter of passersby. Ahmed Masook had been spotted on a boat belonging to an Emirati from UAE. Although not quite royal, the owner was close to some very powerful men in the Middle East. Alex walked towards the *Fair Winds,* curious as to what sort of security the boat might have. With the owner not in residence security might be minimal. That was the best-case scenario.

A beige Maserati convertible with black leather seats was parked beside the steps that led up onto the boat. Alex admired the car. Fast cars were a weakness of his. A young girl ran past him, hair bleached white by the sun, skin tanned as a hazelnut. Her breath was loud and sawing, as if she'd run a long way.

Taylor Masook.

She unhooked a thin chain that hung across the bottom of the steps that led up to the rear deck, darted quickly onboard.

There was no guard visible. No one was on any of the decks Alex could see.

Then angry shouts erupted and echoed off the old, stone walls of the medieval harbor. A girl shrieked. Alex tensed. A tall man with black hair and a heavy beard came into view, dragging Taylor Masook roughly by the arm across the deck.

Ahmed Masook.

Alex stared openly at the commotion along with a couple of other tourists. Ignoring it would look more suspicious.

"How many times have I told you not to leave this boat?" Masook spoke in English. "You are not to play with the local children."

"But I was bored, Daddy! You were gone so long. Josette wasn't here." The girl whined, fighting her father's grip as he pulled her toward the main stateroom.

Who is Josette?

"I told you to stay here and you defied me." The man lost his patience and shook the child. "Do. Not. Defy. Me!"

Alex clamped down hard on the urge to rush up there and punch Masook in the nose and take Taylor straight back to her mother.

Some societies were harsher than others. Any parent would be worried if they thought their child might be in danger. Sometimes that manifested itself in shitty parenting. Alex still wanted to punch the guy in the nose.

The girl cried louder, and the man jerked the kid after him. "I should have left you at home in Dubai."

So, he did live in the UAE. Why *had* Masook brought his kid here when there was an international warrant out for his arrest? Was he really that arrogant that he didn't think he'd be caught, or did he have connections with local cops like Jane suspected?

Alex carried on walking along the pier. He'd seen the shadow of someone moving inside one of the staterooms— probably crew, possibly security. Then there was this mystery "Josette."

Still, it didn't seem as if lifting this child was going to be difficult. In fact, if he hung out at that coffee shop long enough, young Taylor would probably make another excursion when her daddy wasn't looking and Alex could scoop her up off the street. Trouble was, he didn't have time to wait around. Mallory needed him, and he wouldn't leave her for long.

Alex stared out to sea, letting the ocean calm him. Eventually the setting sun told him it was time to head back to the small chateau he'd rented on the edge of town.

He turned and began walking back. A cherry-red Aston Martin coupe weaved in and out of the people walking along the pier, then swung into one of the parking bays opposite another massive yacht. A bulky man with a shaved head got out of the driver's side.

"*Schönes auto.*" Nice car. Alex nodded to him politely. The man gave him a chin lift and then adjusted his suit jacket before heading onto a mega-yacht that looked like a mini cruise ship. The *Akula*. Shark. Alex knew that boat.

He kept strolling along, meandering and taking photographs of everything and anything as his mind whirled. He'd been out of the game for a long time, but he doubted Vladimir Ranich was a *reformed* arms dealer.

What the hell was Vlad doing here in Antibes, and was his presence related to Jane Sanders's ex, or just a nasty coincidence?

CHAPTER FOUR

J ANE STARED AT the small kidney-shaped swimming pool in
the shady courtyard of the small chateau Alex Parker had
rented. Dappled sunlight shimmered on the water, dispersed
by the shade of a large weeping willow. The smell of lavender
permeated the air, and the faint echo of footsteps off old,
cobblestone streets danced delicately over pan tiled roofs.

It should have been idyllic and relaxing, but her fingernails
bit into the tender flesh of her arms, and her teeth clamped
together so fiercely pain shot through her brain. She needed to
know what was happening. Had Alex found Taylor? Was
Ahmed still on the yacht? Was the yacht still in Antibes?

A song thrush flitted into the garden and darted away
when it spotted her standing quietly in the shadows.

Was she doing the right thing in taking a child away from
her father? Would this traumatize Taylor? If so, was it worth
it? Or was Jane being selfish?

What sort of woman abducted her own child? A child she
loved with her whole being, but who probably didn't remember her. Jane's mouth went dry as the thoughts whirled in her
mind. Unanswerable questions. Hopeless dilemmas.

She closed her eyes as if that would somehow eliminate
her doubts and fears.

She wished she could relax, but the knowledge that her

daughter could be close-by made thinking about anything else impossible. If it wasn't for her bodyguard she'd have already gone down to the marina, hoping to catch a peek of her baby. Which was why Alex Parker had assigned her a bodyguard.

Part of her resented Alex for that, but mostly she was just so grateful he was helping her. She didn't know why he'd changed his mind. She didn't care. Her only other option had been going to the *Gendarmerie Nationale* and asking them to execute the warrant for Ahmed's arrest. Something told her her ex-husband wouldn't be here so openly if he didn't have someone on the French police in his pocket. And if Ahmed discovered she was here, if he ever got his hands on her…she was a dead woman.

"Here." A low, male voice made her jump as a glass of iced water appeared in front of her.

She hadn't heard Jack Reilly step into the courtyard. The man moved quietly for such a big guy, not even disturbing the air around him. She took the glass from his hand. "Thank you."

Reilly had strong features, a sharp nose and a stubborn chin. Not pretty, but handsome in a deeply masculine sort of way. So far, he'd been nothing but polite to her.

She took a sip of water, and it slid down her throat in welcome relief. She wiped her lips with the back of her hand. She hadn't even known she was thirsty until she'd started drinking. Alcohol would have been preferable, but Reilly didn't look like the sort who'd approve of her drinking in the daytime.

He looked like the sort of man who followed the rules and never lost control. Jane was good at control, too. Hers masked a level of grief that, when she lost it, reduced her to a pathetic crying mass of hysteria who couldn't function in the real world. But she had to function. She had to survive and be ready to take care of Taylor as soon as she got her child back.

"You should come inside," he said.

She bristled.

Reilly was bulkier than Alex Parker across the shoulders but shared that same dominant male vibe that set her teeth on edge and made her want to run. She met his steady, blue gaze. She was never running again.

"Why?" she asked.

They were alone at the small chateau, which was more a grand house than castle. The staff had left them some food, but Alex had told them their services weren't required and to take the week off. Hopefully they wouldn't be here that long.

She tried not to think about it, but it was possible in less than a week's time she'd have her daughter back—or she might have lost her forever.

She'd bet on Alex Parker any day of the year. Her jaws clamped together, matching the tension in her cramped fingers. Alex was ruthlessly efficient. The scariest thing about him was that he looked so incredibly normal, like a guy you'd want to date. But Jane knew exactly how deadly he could be. Not that Mallory Rooney seemed to mind...

"It's cooler inside," Reilly said reasonably.

He moved as if to touch her, and she swerved to avoid him. "I stopped doing what men thought best for me years ago, Mr. Reilly. So, unless that's a direct order, I'd rather not."

He had lightly tanned skin, military short, dark-blond hair that glinted in the sun, and intelligent blue eyes. His expression didn't alter at her defiant tone, but she got the impression he was trying to figure her out. He had the calm, patient look of a man used to dealing with difficult clients.

"Finish the water, Ms. Sanders. I don't want you collapsing and having to go to the ER and risk being seen."

Taylor was the only thing in the world that mattered to her, and Jane would never jeopardize this mission. So she drank the water, the slide of it quenching her parched throat.

Reilly reached out for the glass, and she handed it back. Their fingers brushed, and an electric shock jumped across the connection. Her eyes shot to his, and she saw his pupils flare in reaction even though the rest of his expression remained implacable. She was surprised that her body had responded that way to a man when her mind was so focused on her daughter. She hated that it betrayed her with something as basic as physical attraction.

Maybe this was why the universe had punished her. For being such a terrible mother.

Reilly shifted his stance. Clearly, he was going to stand there all day until she gave in to his commands. She didn't like him bossing her around. She didn't like being dominated. She didn't like that tiny ember of attraction that had flared to life out of the cold wasteland of her heart. She needed Jack Reilly to leave her alone, and she knew exactly how to make him do it.

"Was there something else you wanted?" she asked suggestively, giving him a thorough once over.

He took a step back as she'd known he would. Jack Reilly was not the sort of guy to fool around on the job.

She moved toward him, and he retreated a second step and then stood his ground as if remembering he was the one who was armed and dangerous. Baiting him beat staring at the reflection of light on the water and wondering if her daughter would remember her. The sooner he left her alone the happier they'd both be. She ran her hand over the warm cotton of his shirt front and felt his muscles ripple in response.

He grabbed her wrist with the hand that wasn't holding the empty glass of water. "Ms. Sanders," he warned.

"Jane," she insisted. He smelled warm and male and wore some tangy aftershave that teased her senses.

"What are you doing?" His eyes narrowed as he stared down at her.

"Your job is to watch my every move and make sure I don't run down to the yacht club, correct?" She didn't wait for an answer. She wanted to shock him into keeping his distance. "You could do that much more easily if we were both naked."

His lips firmed in disapproval, which unexpectedly made tears prick her eyes.

Making someone hate you was easy, it just took a few bold or bitchy moves. She slowly moved her hand lower, letting her fingers drift over the front of his pants, giving him plenty of opportunity to avoid her touch. Testosterone practically oozed off him. There was no way he'd take this sort of treatment lying down.

"Why, Mr. Reilly. I do believe you think my idea has merit." She didn't stop stroking him, and he didn't move away, though his eyes slitted further and his nostrils flared. The fingers around her one wrist tightened another notch.

"Ms. Sanders," he warned again.

"Jane." She curled her fingers around his impressive length and an ache began to throb between her thighs. The spark of desire took her by surprise. Over the years, she'd often used sex as a distraction from the ugly emptiness of her life, but she hadn't expected to feel pleasure from this.

31

Reilly gently tossed the empty glass onto the nearby couch, then caught her other wrist and pulled her hand away from him.

She pouted appropriately.

"*Ms. Sanders.*" His blue eyes were dark now, heated, and she thought for one wild crazy moment he might kiss her. "You're a client." He let go of her wrists and took a step back. "I don't have relations with clients." He snatched up the glass and started to walk away, but not before she noticed the tented front of his pants.

"I don't want *relations*, Mr. Reilly." Her voice cracked. Embarrassed by the hint of vulnerability she'd revealed, she added, "I was just offering to let you fuck me hard against a wall."

He stopped and looked at her over his shoulder. His eyes ran down her body with appreciation. They weren't cold, and they weren't full of loathing the way she'd expected them to be.

"I don't fuck clients against the wall. I don't fuck clients anywhere." His voice softened. "I know you're hurting." Suddenly the pain in her heart caught fire. "I know you're worried about your daughter. There are other ways to deal with those emotions."

"I don't want to *deal* with my emotions any other way," she snarled.

He blew out a quiet breath, and his eyes crinkled. "Yeah, I got the self-destruct message loud and clear."

She flinched and looked away as shame washed over her. It was easy to get people to hate you. Getting someone to like you was so much harder, as she knew from far too much personal experience.

"You aren't in a good place to be making important decisions like who to have sex with, Ms. Sanders, and I cannot afford to be distracted by a beautiful woman."

Beautiful? Her eyes shot to his, and her mouth fell open in surprise. She hadn't thought of herself as beautiful in years. She felt ugly, scarred, and twisted. Look at how she'd handled a man kind enough to bring her a glass of water on a hot day? All because inside she was being shredded slowly through a meat grinder. He hadn't deserved that. Jack Reilly had been nothing except professional and courteous.

God, she was pathetic.

She hadn't always been such a bitch. There had been a time when she'd been kind, too. She'd been kind even after she'd had the crap beaten out of her on a regular basis by a man she thought had loved her. It was only after he'd stolen her child that the black rot of bitterness had seeped in. Seeped in and drowned every good thing about her.

She held Reilly's blue gaze as she drew in a long, deep breath. "I'm sorry. I was offensive and rude, Mr. Reilly. That's not really who I am." She swallowed. At least it wasn't who she wanted to be. "It won't happen again."

The understanding in his gaze made her want to weep. "I'm a big boy, Jane. I can deal." He grinned, and his face transformed.

She laughed because he referred to both his maturity and the size of his erection without any other comment being necessary. A man comfortable and confident in his own skin.

"You didn't offend me. Just gave hope to an underutilized piece of my anatomy," he said.

She seriously doubted that. She cleared her throat. "Thank you, Mr. Reilly. I promise I won't touch you inappropriately again." *Thank you for not taking advantage of what I so clearly offered. Thank you for distracting me. Thank you for not hating me even though I wanted you to.*

"Call me Reilly, or Jack. Mr. Reilly is my father."

"Isn't that a little familiar between bodyguard and client?" she teased softly.

He carefully adjusted the front of his pants. "It's about as familiar as I get on the job," he admitted. "The exception being a few minutes ago." He glanced up at the hot sun. "Don't be outside too long. You're beginning to burn."

She lifted her chin as he gave her another long look before heading inside.

It had been years since anyone had given a damn about something as simple as whether or not she burnt in the sun. She looked up at the cloudless, blue sky. She'd gotten rid of him like she'd planned, but it didn't feel as good as she'd expected.

She didn't deserve his kindness, but he provided it anyway. She swallowed the uncomfortable knot that formed in her throat. Even if she never saw her child again, she was going to start being the parent her daughter deserved, the sort of person a child might be proud of. Kind. Brave. Compassionate.

Her ex would not destroy her. No matter what happened he would not destroy her.

CHAPTER FIVE

WHEN ALEX GOT back to the chateau it was dark outside, and Jane was waiting for him in the lounge.

She stood as he came in the door. "What happened? Did you see her?"

He kept walking toward her, and she started backing up until she hit the wall. She closed her eyes, clearly bracing for a blow.

Alex stilled as he realized the truth behind Jane's coldness.

"Jane," he said softly, gently.

Her face crumpled as if she knew she'd revealed her secret.

It cracked something inside him to think someone had abused this woman. Her icy exterior wasn't superiority the way he'd always supposed. It was a means of keeping the world at bay. Of keeping her pain hidden and her body safe.

"Sorry," she gasped in a deep, shuddering breath and then whispered, "most of the time I can pretend it never happened." She crossed her arms over her chest and met his gaze. "You always scare me to my bones. I guess you brought it all back."

It was his turn to flinch. He knew she thought he was a monster. That's why she'd come to him for help in the first place.

"What business was Masook in?" Alex asked.

Blue eyes were confused as she frowned at him. She was so

brittle and composed he wondered she didn't break. But she held his gaze so they were making progress.

"When I met him he said his family was in construction." Her mouth pinched. "I never actually saw him do any work."

"One of the idle rich?" Alex mused. He didn't think Masook was idle, though. He'd bet money the man was just furtive about conducting business that was both lucrative and highly illegal.

Jane moved away from him and picked up a bottle of wine and poured out a large glass. She held up the bottle. "Would you like one?"

Alex shook his head. "Tell me about him. How did you two meet?"

"In Florida at some charity function." She took a big gulp of wine and put the glass down on the coffee table. She sat abruptly. Condensation gathered on the outside of the glass, and she stroked her finger along the stem. "I can't lie. His being rich was one of the main things that first attracted me to him. So, it's my own fault. Don't they say people who marry for money earn every penny?"

She gave another cynical laugh, and Alex felt his mouth go dry. He'd only ever guessed at half of her source of pain.

"I come from a family with deep roots in the south. We knew how to spend money, we just didn't know how to work for it." Something changed in her eyes. "At first Ahmed was kind and attentive and showered me in diamonds. I thought I'd hit the jackpot. I fell in love. We got married and I became pregnant straight away, which hadn't been part of the plan for either of us." Her lips wobbled. "Then I had Taylor and I fell madly in love with my little girl. My mom and I were never close, so it was unexpected." She wiped beneath her eyes, pretending she wasn't crying. "Wait until your child arrives."

"I already know." The love he felt for his and Mallory's unborn baby was equaled only by the love he felt for Mallory.

She shook her head. "No. You *think* you know. You've had a glimpse of it, but it's the tip of the iceberg compared to what's coming. When you hold them, when you smell the scent of their skin and look into their trusting eyes. They smile at you, and it's like another universe opens up." Her eyes met his. Tragic. Anguished. "They own you."

He wasn't sure he'd survive feeling even more for the woman he loved or the child she carried.

"Ahmed didn't like me spending more time with Taylor than with him. He became jealous of his own daughter." She picked up her wine again with a shaking hand and took another big gulp. It was a dangerous way to numb reality but there were worse methods. "That's why he stole her when I left him. Because he knew that would cause me the most pain."

Alex forced the pity from his heart. Pity wasn't what she wanted from him. "Come with me. I want you to look at a photograph of a man." He went to his bedroom, and she followed cautiously as he unlocked his suitcase. Alex removed his laptop and started it up.

He searched the internet for a photograph of Vladimir Ranich without any accompanying details. It wasn't easy to find, but Alex knew where to look.

He turned the screen toward Jane. "Did Masook ever do business with this man?"

She had her hands crossed over her chest and leaned forward from the waist rather than stepping closer to him. Her mouth prepared to form the word "no" until she actually looked at the image.

"Oh. Yes. I remember him coming to Ahmed's house in Saudi Arabia once." She shook her head. "I didn't actually meet him, and I don't know if he was there for business or pleasure. I was chasing Taylor around the foyer when he arrived." Her gaze drifted as she lost herself in memories. "We weren't introduced. It was just before Ahmed let me take Taylor back to the States to visit my parents. I was busy pretending to be crazy in love with him even though he liked to beat me unconscious at least once a month." She touched her rib as if a ghost pain still lingered. Alex had that, too. Phantom symptoms of times he'd rather forget.

"Taylor was two. I knew I had to make him believe I'd never leave him. I told him I didn't want to go back to the US, that I needed stay with him. He slapped me and ordered the servants to pack." She smiled a cold, brittle smile of triumph that immediately slid into despair. "He got his revenge when he stole Taylor and ran." She huddled into herself. "The only positive thing was I got away from him. He would have killed me if I'd stayed. He'll still kill me if he catches me now."

Not on Alex's watch.

Masook hadn't been on the CIA's radar. Maybe that had changed since Alex had left the agency. Maybe Masook was the real reason The Gateway Project had targeted Jane Sanders in the first place.

"Looking back, he arranged the trip for me very quickly and never imagined I'd bolt from such a *loving* husband." Her eyes sharpened. "Who is the guy in the photograph and why are you asking? Is he involved with Ahmed? Did you see Taylor? Is she okay?" The words ran together as panic overtook her.

"I saw Taylor."

Jane stopped talking, and her eyes got huge. Her hand clenched and unclenched. "How did she look? Did she look happy? How tall is she?"

Alex pressed his lips together and gave her an approximation of the girl's height. Jane's face turned anguished at all the years that represented.

"Her father was telling her off for sneaking off the boat and playing with the local kids without permission."

Jane blanched. "Did he hit her?"

Alex shook his head. "I didn't see him raise his hand to her. I did see him shake her. I don't know for sure what happened when they went inside."

Her eyes darted around the room without seeing it. "I never saw him hit anyone else. Only me. I have held onto that hope ever since the day he took her." She stared off into space for a moment, then her mind seemed to snap back into place and she pointed at the image of Vladimir Ranch on the screen. "Who is this man? What does he have to do with Ahmed?" she asked again.

Alex pressed his lips together. "I don't know yet."

She eyed him like she knew he was lying. "What was security like?"

"Minimal."

"Are you going back tonight?" She looked so hopeful Alex wanted to lie to her.

"No. Not tonight. I want to do more recon. First, I need some sleep." He needed to talk to Frazer.

She blinked and seemed to become aware she was in his bedroom. She backed away. "Sorry. I'll leave you alone."

All the years they'd worked together and they'd never really trusted one another. They'd both been trapped doing something they hated and had hoarded their secret pain. He was no longer that person. He didn't want to dislike her anymore.

"What made you do it? Work for The Gateway Project?" he asked quietly, so Reilly wouldn't accidentally overhear them.

She gave a shuddering breath and whispered back. "They told me they'd bring her home to me. Taylor. They said that if I gave them three years of my life they'd make sure Taylor came home and Ahmed wouldn't be able to find me. Ever. I was three months away from that when…"

When it had all crashed down around their heads.

"There was no guarantee they'd have kept their promise," Alex said gently. "You know that, right?"

She nodded slowly. "Yes. But some hope was better than none."

There was always hope. Always. Even when things looked horrifically bleak. He gave her a soft smile. "We'll get her back."

She swallowed hard as if choking down a sob and walked swiftly away.

Reilly appeared in the doorway.

"Any problems today?" Alex asked.

Reilly shook his head. "You really gonna get the kid back?"

"I'm gonna try. Just keep Jane occupied, okay? It's not going to be as straightforward as I'd hoped. Certain unforeseen things have come up."

Reilly cocked a brow. "*Things*?"

"Individuals. Dangerous individuals."

"Is the child in danger?" Reilly asked quietly.

"I don't believe so, but I can't afford for Jane to get involved in this. She's a wildcard. Keep her contained, even if you have to chain her to the bed."

Something flickered across Reilly's features and then was gone. "Roger that. I'll keep her out of trouble."

Alex just hoped he could do the same.

CHAPTER SIX

"W HERE THE HELL are you?" Frazer asked testily.

"You mean on a lazy Saturday morning?" Alex answered casually. It was already evening in the south of France, of course. He'd made a decision and needed Frazer's help. If Jane found out, she'd gut him, and he wasn't sure he'd blame her.

The audible equivalent of an eye roll came down the line. "I was going to organize a few drinks tonight. Figured that was part of my best man duties."

Alex laughed. "You going to try and get me drunk?"

"Don't be ridiculous." Frazer mocked. "But there is a bar at the academy."

Alex and Frazer both had too many enemies and too many trust issues to get hammered in a bar anywhere except maybe the FBI's National Academy. No way in hell would either of them get drunk there.

"No strippers?" Truthfully Alex hadn't even thought about a bachelor party. It seemed too normal for a man like him.

Frazer grunted. "Rooney would kill me. So would Izzy."

"So would I." Strippers held little appeal when you were in love with a smart, beautiful woman. "I should have organized a trip down to Haley's private island for the weekend," Alex said. The men who'd attacked Patrick Killion and Audrey

Lockhart had been removed and repatriated months ago. Haley still didn't know exactly what had happened, but she had asked about the bullet holes in the front door. Alex was glad they'd never breached the main house. Haley would have strung him up by his balls if it had been damaged.

"I hadn't planned any strippers, but I did round up a couple of the guys to come over tonight for a few beers and some steak. When can you get here?"

Alex hesitated. "Something came up."

He sensed the moment Frazer's focus shifted. "How so?"

"You at your laptop?"

"I'm sitting on my deck with a beer. Izzy is insisting on making me brunch before she catches a flight to OBX to close on her houses. Kit's going with her and they're driving back in Kit's car—alone." Disapproval dripped from Frazer's tone.

Alex understood it. It was disgruntlement that they couldn't wrap the people they loved in cotton wool. Dissatisfaction they couldn't force the world to their will.

"Izzy and Kit can take care of themselves. They should be fine." Frazer's girlfriend was a former Army captain and routinely carried a Glock. Alex liked her. She was reserved. Alex was reserved, too. People with secrets generally were. She and Lincoln Frazer were perfect for one another.

"I know she *should* be fine. Doesn't stop me from thinking about all the bad things that could happen." Frazer's tone was beyond pissed and made Alex smile. He sympathized. He really did. Unfortunately, they didn't get to make all the rules when it came to the women they loved.

"What's up?" Frazer asked with a sigh.

"I'm going to send you two photographs." Alex hit send and carried on talking. "The one guy's name is Vladimir

Ranich. The second is Ahmed Masook."

"Jane Sander's ex."

"Yes."

It made sense that Frazer had checked Jane out. He'd checked out everybody associated with The Gateway Project.

"Alex," Frazer finally drew out, "where did you get these images?"

Time to 'fess up. "I took them this afternoon in Antibes."

There was a long-suffering sigh. "I know you aren't *working*—so what's going on?"

Alex expelled a breath he hadn't realized he'd been holding. When Frazer said "working" he wasn't talking cybersecurity. "If I was *working* I wouldn't tell you, you know that, right?"

Frazer laughed. "I know you better than that, Alex. You asked me to be best man for a reason."

It was humbling to realize Frazer trusted him even though Alex had killed more people than most serial killers. Death was often the most effective solution to a serious problem, but Alex couldn't do it anymore. He couldn't pass judgment or carry out a sentence for other people's misdeeds. Not unless someone forced his hand.

"You know you're getting married next weekend, right?" Frazer said drolly. "You need to get a move on and tell me what's going on."

Alex glanced at the door. Jane and Reilly were both sleeping. He'd set up a basic alarm system that would alert him to intruders or to anyone trying to leave the property. He didn't trust Jane's ability to resist spying on her child. He'd swept for bugs. Twice.

"Jane discovered Masook was in Antibes and that he'd

brought their daughter with him."

"So, let Interpol serve the arrest warrant," said Frazer reasonably.

"Jane thinks he'll have paid off enough local cops to receive a warning and flee. If that happens she'll never see her daughter again."

Frazer huffed. "So, she asked you to help her?"

"I said no."

"And yet there you are."

"She was gonna try and do this herself." Alex let out a frustrated breath and ran his hand through his short hair. "She played by the rules, Linc. She went through the court system and allowed Masook to see his child even though she must have hated taking that risk. And he fucked her over. Gave the legal system the bird because he's a rich asshole and thinks the rules don't apply to him." His voice vibrated with anger.

"And you're such a fan of rules. What else?"

"He hit her."

Silence on the other end of the line. Violence was common in their business, but there was something particularly wretched about a man hitting his wife.

"Tell me about this other guy Ranich," said Frazer.

"When I was working for the agency he was funneling weapons from old soviet military installations into the black market. I showed Jane a photograph and she said she'd seen Ranich at Masook's house once, but she doesn't know anything about him and hadn't been introduced."

"You believe her?"

"Yes, I do."

"So, you think Vladimir Ranich is selling arms to Ahmed Masook?"

"Not necessarily. But I am sure Masook's legitimate businesses don't make enough money for him to live the way he does, and it seems like a hell of a coincidence they just happen to be here at the same time."

Frazer groaned. He knew this was too big for either of them to ignore.

"Ranich might also be looking to *buy* something for the Russians." Alex thought about the woman who'd watched him in the cafe. She might have been attracted by his devilish good looks, but his spidey senses had pinged way too fervently for that. "I think the Agency *might* be involved. And if not Five Eyes or Israel, then possibly France or Germany."

"Ah, hell." Frazer wasn't making him feel any better.

"If I go in and grab the kid then I might fuck up an operation. But if our intelligence agencies aren't involved, or the ICs of our allies aren't involved…"

"Then they should be. But bringing them into the loop ruins your chance of grabbing the kid." Frazer swore. "Why do you always make things complicated?"

"It's a gift," Alex said. "Look, I'm going to go back to the marina to see what I can discover, but if you don't hear from me for a few days…"

"Oh, no. Nope. You called me. Now we're doing this my way," Frazer told him.

"Only if you can guarantee getting the kid back and me getting home in time to marry the woman of my dreams."

They both knew that in this sort of situation there were no guarantees. Frazer swore colorfully. Frazer didn't usually get flustered, but being a best man had clearly upset his equilibrium.

Alex heard him talking to someone before coming back on

the line. "Don't do anything until you hear from me, understand? I've a few contacts I can leverage, but if there's an illegal arms deals going down we need to know about it."

"That's why I called you." And why, if she found out, Jane Sanders would have Alex's head.

CHAPTER SEVEN

MONDAY MORNING, ALEX was back at that same cafe, reading another copy of *Die Zeit*, drinking another cappuccino and slowly going out of his ever-loving mind. Today he wore a pale blue, linen shirt, cream, linen pants and a white, straw fedora and dark sunglasses. He missed his jeans. He missed his combat boots. He missed Mallory more.

The good news was he'd written one-hundred place names on customized white cards in his best handwriting. The bad news was he still had another hundred to go. He'd run background checks on everyone attending their wedding and some of the guests he wouldn't let look after his potted plants. But they were friends of the senator's or the judge's and, apparently, the groom didn't get a say. He'd hired another firm to provide security as an added precaution. He wasn't expecting trouble, but neither was he taking any chances.

Frazer had gone dark, which wasn't like the guy. Alex needed to make a decision about whether or not to fulfill his primary objective and grab the kid, or pursue this new angle. Putting arms dealers out of business wasn't his job anymore, but defeating terrorism was everyone's problem. No one got a free pass.

Jane was getting antsy. Reilly had his hands full trying to keep her occupied and contained.

Alex had spent the last day or so gathering information. He'd run facial recognition programs on images he'd captured while strolling the streets and bars of Antibes and come up with a few more potential bad guys.

It was the people who weren't on the IC radar who worried him most—they were the people they needed to identify and shut down.

His cell rang, and he answered with an internal grin. Mallory. She was up late. He wondered how her German was. "*Hallo.*"

"Hey. Can you talk? How's everything going?"

"*Es geht mir gut.*"

A few beats of confused silence. "I thought you were in France."

"*Richtig.*"

She groaned. "I don't speak German. I'm gonna text you."

"*Gute idee. Auf wiederhören, fräulein.*"

"I love you."

The best words in any language. Alex resisted the urge to say it back. He had a role to play and that role was of a happily married man. He kept one eye on the quay and texted Mal who was listed under MR with a picture of another woman. The communications were encrypted but it was always possible if someone captured Alex they could eventually force him to open his phone. Everyone broke under torture. The key was gaining enough time that appropriate safeguards could be put into place to mitigate potential damage. Frazer would look after Mal if anything happened to him. Alex didn't doubt that.

Not that he intended to get caught.

Alex: *Why are you up so late?*

MR: *Couldn't sleep. Junior is kicking.*

Alex: *Everything alright?*

MR: *Everything is *fine**

After the scare Mal had on New Year's Eve, Alex would never take their health for granted. But he refused to obsess. Even as he obsessed, he refused to obsess. It was an ongoing process.

Alex: *How was your last weekend as a free woman?*

MR: *How was your last weekend as a free man?*

Alex: *Sucked because you weren't here.*

MR: *Awwww…*

Alex: *Did Haley get your friends drunk?*

MR: *Ha! You have no idea how much Harvard law students drink.*

Alex: *Are you saying they drank more than Haley?*

MR: *…No, but my mother did. I needed the stripper's help to get Haley into bed.*

Alex: *Wait.*

Alex: *What?*

Alex: *Stripper???*

MR: *Actually, three strippers but only one helped me get Haley into bed.*

Alex: *You had three strippers at your bachelorette party? In a health spa? And you were in a bedroom with one of them?*

MR: *They didn't go full monty despite my mother offering them a thousand-dollar tip if they did.*

Alex: *But…*

MR: Not my idea!!!

Alex blinked stupidly at his cell.

Alex: I'm now terrified of your mother. Glad they kept their shorts on. Would have hated to have to kill them all...

MR: Who said it was their shorts they kept on? ;)

Alex laughed. He never forgot how blessed he was to have found this woman, or the knowledge that she trusted him. It humbled him.

MR: I have to go. I love you. Keep safe. Don't be late!

Alex: I'll be there. I'm just off to find some strippers for my impromptu bucks night...

MR: You're not the only one with a gun, buster.

Alex: :)

The fact he was sitting here smiley-face emoticoning his pregnant fiancée was not lost on him. His life had gone from doom and gloom to almost too good to be true. He didn't intend to fuck it up.

Something bright caught his eye. The flaxen tresses of a slight figure hurrying along the quay. Little Taylor Masook. His fingers tensed on the handle of his coffee mug. This was a perfect opportunity to spirit her away. Would she fight him? Would he need to subdue her? Not a happy thought. But he could do it.

Or did he wait for Frazer?

He climbed to his feet, and the little girl glanced toward him and started waving frantically.

He froze. Had he been made? By a frickin' eight-year-old?

"Josette!" she shouted.

Alex turned and saw the beautiful, young woman he'd observed on Saturday sitting at a table against the wall. He hadn't noticed her arrival because he'd been distracted talking to Mal.

Fuck. That's how operatives died.

The woman caught his gaze for a brief second before her eyes slipped to the child. So, *this* was Josette. She must be the nanny or a tutor. Perhaps she was the reason Masook had brought the child with him. Because if the child was close, so was the nanny? A man as insecure as Masook probably wouldn't want to stray far from this woman if she was his lover. And if she wasn't, then this would be a good opportunity to try and change that fact.

Alex put some euros on the table, weighed down with his cup. Then he headed inside on the pretext of using the bathroom. He stood at the counter checking out the cake selection as Josette climbed to her feet and went to meet the girl at the edge of the patio. Alex took a quick photograph of the woman and the child through the window. He sent the image to Frazer and his team back in DC.

From what he could gather from Taylor's animated arm-waving and high-pitched excitement her daddy wanted Josette back on the boat ASAP. Probably meant he was going somewhere and didn't want Taylor's company but didn't want to leave the kid alone. If Alex's primary objective had still been to grab the kid, then the next couple of hours would have been the ideal time to do that. Jane would get her daughter back, Alex would make it to his own wedding.

He eyed the blue-eyed, blonde child as she spoke earnestly

to Josette. He could see her mother in her coloring and the shape of her face. The slice of her nose was her father's.

Ahmed Masook had forfeited a father's rights when he'd lifted his fists to his wife, and again when he'd flouted the US court order. If Alex's gut was correct then Ahmed Masook was also an arms broker, and they were some of the dirtiest scum in the universe. They didn't care where weapons ended up. They just cared about their personal wealth. A kid shouldn't be within a mile of that sort of evil.

Admittedly, some might say the same thing about him.

Josette went back to the table and collected her things and followed Taylor out of the patio and back along the quay.

It was another beautiful day on the Med. Alex followed slowly, losing them in the crowd ahead, but not worried. He knew where they were going. He mingled with tourists as they took in the opulence of the setting and the fancy yachts. He drew in the sharp scent of the ocean and enjoyed the heat of the sun on his skin. Even so, he'd rather have been in Virginia or DC on a cool spring day with Mal by his side.

He glanced at *Fair Winds* and the *Akula* with admiration and awe he wasn't really feeling. These people expected gawkers and probably ignored them. There was a helicopter landing pad on both boats complete with machines that gleamed in the sunshine like giant metal wasps.

He passed a man smoking a cigar and wearing a cerulean silk suit. Alex kept his pace to a saunter, but his heart gave a jolt.

Serat Al-Hadam was a front man for the Iranians.

What the hell was Masook brokering?

The former Soviet Union had been rife with nuclear, bio-logical and chemical arsenals when it had fallen and, with the tacit approval of the Russian government, men like Ranich had been lining their pockets selling off those instruments of death ever since.

The full heat of the midday sun hit him as he approached the end of Millionaires' Quay. Something was going down. Something big. An international arms deal was too big to ignore, but so was his promise to help Jane get her daughter back.

Jane was trying to move on with her life. The same way he was. Images bombarded him. Not of the men he'd killed, but friends and patriots who'd died in service, innocent civilians running the gauntlet of warlords and governments as they tried to live normal lives between power grabs.

Only a month ago a white nationalist had tried to bring some homemade devastation to the heart of DC. What would happen if one of these bastards got hold of some bonafide military-grade hardware, or some other weapon of mass destruction?

He stood on the end of the pier, struggling with his options, trying to figure out which was more important—getting an innocent child away from a cesspit, or making sure everyone involved in this arms deal was scooped up and put out of business.

Unfortunately, he knew the answer and that was another blow for Jane Sanders's hopes.

Another massive yacht entered the port. It was three stories high, and the sun gleamed off the white hull so intensely Alex squinted and shielded his eyes from the glare. And there, on the very top deck, stood a guy who would have looked just like Lincoln Frazer except for the scruff on his jaw and the board shorts he was wearing. That, and the fact he was kissing the crap out of a woman who looked exactly like Ashley Chen.

Alex turned away to face the deep blue of the Med.

He smiled.

The cavalry had arrived.

CHAPTER EIGHT

FRAZER IGNORED LUCAS Randall's silent glower as he walked back into the main living area of billionaire financier Robin Greenburg's enormous luxury yacht, *Ascension*. He still held Agent Chen's hand as if he had every intention of dragging her off to bed and making mad, passionate love to her. As soon as he was sure no one on the outside could see them he let go of her hand and raised his brow at Lucas.

Ashley was posing as his lover, and Lucas was going to have to get used to him having his hands on her for the next day or so. They'd needed Ashley's technical genius onboard this vessel and having a woman running around in a bikini was good cover. Foolishly, few considered them a threat.

Lucas was posing as crew, as was Patrick Killion and a couple of Brits that Killion assured him were trustworthy. This mission was an off the books joint CIA/FBI operation with full cooperation from Interpol. The only member of Greenburg's real crew was the captain who Robin assured him was trustworthy and closed-mouthed.

He'd better be.

Years ago, Frazer had saved Greenburg's life by arresting the man's then wife who—unbeknownst to Greenburg—had already disposed of three husbands before she'd gotten her razor-sharp talons into what she must have thought of as the motherlode. At first the guy hadn't believed Frazer and had threatened to destroy his career. Then Frazer let Greenburg watch him interview the woman. The evidence Frazer had was overwhelming and it hadn't taken long until she'd confessed to the murders in exchange for avoiding the death penalty. Then she'd told Frazer in minute detail how she'd planned to get Robin drunk and push him overboard on one of their moonlit cruises.

Who said romance was dead?

Frazer regularly took advantage of the guy's gratitude and media interests to strategically aid FBI cases.

It was ironic that over the years the billionaire had invited him onto this boat dozens of times. Frazer had never had the time, nor the inclination, to indulge in this sort of vacation. But now he needed the vessel to blend in with the other paragons of opulent wealth.

Greenburg was off on some Australian outback adventure, and the boat had been moored in Monaco, thank god. It was perfect cover for Millionaires' Quay and allowed them to bring in all the necessary equipment and firearms they might need— kindly provided by the CIA who was eager to jump on this unexpected, but solid intel.

"Matt and Scarlett are in place," Lucas told him, staring out the window toward one of the smaller quays.

Frazer checked them out with binocs. Sure enough, the two lovebirds were on the tiny deck of the small sailboat they'd rented. Scarlett sat cross-legged sipping from a mug and Matt was showing off his muscles as he stretched out on the deck.

Once it got dark, Matt Lazlo, a former Navy SEAL, would attach some hi-tech listening devices to the hulls of mega-yachts. Scarlett Stone was a physics genius who added some nice color to Matt's cover. More importantly, Scarlett had been developing her own virtually undetectable listening devices. As sea water created serious problems for radio signals Frazer had asked her to help them out. Matt hadn't been happy, but nothing bad would happen to Scarlett. The two of them would work independently from the rest of the team. They planned to leave on tomorrow's high tide.

Ashley sat down and started typing on her laptop.

"Alex was on the pier. Did you see him?" Frazer asked Lucas.

Lucas nodded.

"I didn't see a thing." Ashley admitted. She was still nervous around Frazer, but she'd turned out to be an excellent behavioral scientist with computer skills that allowed them to dig deep into the unchartered waters of the dark web.

"Probably because someone was sucking your face," Lucas said dryly.

"It's a hard job but someone's got to do it." Patrick Killion joined them in the lounge and gave Frazer his trademark shit-eating grin.

Frazer quirked a brow. Kissing Agent Chen, while not a chore, certainly wasn't something he'd want to do for any reason besides work. "I'm going to head into town with Killion and wait for Alex to find us. You guys see what you can pick up or observe from here. If you're a good boy," Frazer eyed Lucas, "I'll let you sleep in the main stateroom with one of the other agents tonight."

"Pretty sure *I'm* the one who decides who gets to sleep with me," Ashley commented.

Lucas grinned.

Frazer nodded. *Touché.* "Don't go breaking cover while I'm away."

Ashley snorted. "Yeah, I think I've got the undercover thing down pat. See you in a few."

Frazer's main priority was still getting the groom-to-be to the church on time without any bullet wounds or arrest warrants. He changed into jeans and button-down white shirt and flip flops, which felt weird on his feet.

It had taken some doing to arrange this op on the fly, but everything had come together nicely.

They were going to find out what these bastards were selling, who the potential buyers were, and on top of that, they were going to retrieve the Masook child to go live with her mother—her legal guardian. Then they were all going to go home because they had a wedding to attend. A wedding he didn't intend to miss.

CHAPTER NINE

Reilly watched Jane reach for the bottle of wine from the fridge even though it was only noon. She paused for a moment in the middle of the enormous kitchen with its flagstone floor, then silently put the bottle back.

She turned and caught him watching her. She was wearing jeans and a blue t-shirt today, no make-up, her hair tied back in a simple ponytail. It was the first time he'd seen her looking less than perfectly packaged. He liked it. He liked it a lot.

She gave him a tired smile. "Don't look so proud of me. I've used alcohol and sex to get through the loss of Taylor in the past. Both are very effective in the moment." Her voice was pure southern belle and almost as sweet as her face. "But you already rejected the latter and I'm vetoing the former in case Alex brings Taylor home today." Her features tightened. "I don't want her thinking I'm a lush."

Her words took him back to their encounter a few days ago when she'd touched him and he'd wanted to strip her naked and christen the pool. But she was his client. He did not mess with clients.

"You're not a lush," he said quietly.

Humor flashed in her eyes along with enough heat to tell him she meant what she said. "I'm not a whore either, but it doesn't mean I don't like sex."

Damn. He didn't want to talk about sex, especially after his boss told him to do whatever it took to distract her.

"With the right man, I happen to like it a lot." Her teeth bit into her bottom lip, and her gaze drifted down his body. Reilly felt a corresponding response in his dick.

"We can play cards," he suggested a little desperately.

Her eyes crinkled at the corners, and he thought he saw a touch of admiration in their depths. "Not a lot of men would turn down a blowjob for a game of cards."

His pulse sped up, and his skin felt scorched, but he forced himself not to react. "Under normal circumstances in a choice between a hand of poker and having your mouth on me? I'd definitely want your mouth." He made it personal. He made it about him and her, not some anonymous ejaculate down a stranger's throat. "But I am not the jerk who takes advantage of a woman under difficult circumstances."

Her lips curved, and her eyes darkened. He found himself wishing he could bend the rules once, just to taste her.

"I think I'm the one taking advantage, Jack."

And he wanted her to. He really did. But he couldn't. He couldn't cross that line.

He pulled a pack of cards from his pocket. "Poker or Crazy Eights?"

"Strip poker?" She raised a mocking brow.

He'd walked right into that one. He shook his head ruefully.

She grew serious and looked at him for a long moment until the grip she had on her own arms lessened. "If something doesn't happen soon I think I might go insane," she admitted tightly.

"I'm not going to let you. We're in this together until you

get your daughter back."

"It's been four years."

The desolation in her eyes got to him. "Alex has got this," he reminded her.

She slowly released a tense breath. Finally, she nodded. "Crazy Eights it is."

CHAPTER TEN

F RAZER AND KILLION found a bar in the center of the old town and ordered two bottles of blond beer.

Killion watched the door. Frazer kept an eye on the rear exit. They'd chosen a spot near a small, indoor fountain, which helped destroy the quality of intercepts in the unlikely event someone was listening in.

Killion was here because Alex had helped him and Audrey Lockhart out of a jam in January and now he was returning the favor.

They clinked bottles.

"Here's to retirement." Killion grinned.

Frazer took a long swallow and wiped his mouth, startled by the feel of bristles on his jaw. It made him look less like a Fed, and more relaxed and carefree than he'd ever actually be. He hoped he got to find out what Izzy thought of it before he shaved. He checked the time. She'd be asleep. She was staying with her uncle Ted before starting the drive back in the morning. Ted had volunteered to load all their personal belongings and any furniture they wanted to keep into a moving van, and drive it north at the end of the month. Frazer wasn't used to having so many people in his life but he was adjusting. He was enjoying the simple pleasure of having someone to talk to at the end of a grueling day. Someone to wake up with every morning. Someone to make love to whenever they had a spare five minutes alone...

"How's retirement working out for you?" Frazer asked the spook.

Killion cocked a brow as he sprawled in his seat. "Good in terms of remembering how to be a decent human being, but if I don't go back to work soon I have a feeling Audrey might start grinding a little frog skin into my breakfast smoothies."

Killion's better half studied one of the most toxic creatures on earth—poison dart frogs.

"*El cartel de Manos de Dios* is done chasing her, right? The danger is over?"

Killion nodded. "She's safe, but I've told her that no way is she returning to Colombia, which made her kind of mad." Then he gave a long-suffering sigh, but Frazer wasn't fooled. The guy adored Audrey's feistiness and independence.

Killion played with the label around the neck of the beer bottle. "They want me to run the Farm."

Frazer's brows skipped high. The Farm was the CIA's training facility at Camp Peary, Virginia.

That was a big deal.

"You gonna do it?" Killion pissed people off on a regular basis, but those who cared to look beyond the cocky, cynical veneer discovered the integrity of the man and a depth of unwavering service. Someone somewhere must have recognized that.

Killion shrugged. You'd be forgiven for believing he hadn't given it much thought. Frazer knew better.

"The powers-that-be offered to set Audrey up in her own private lab facility but she says she wants to work in a university setting. Says it feeds her thirst for knowledge. There

are enough colleges in Virginia we could make it work."
Killion shrugged again. "We haven't figured out the future yet.
I'm still on leave. I took six months off. I needed a sanity
break." Killion could talk the hind legs off an elephant, he just
rarely talked about himself or his emotions—or his *sanity*.

Most of the time, people like Frazer and Killion pretended
not to have emotions or lives outside the office. It was a
miracle any of them had found a person willing to take a
chance on them. They were all a little bit warped. A little bit
jagged. A little bit damaged.

Alex pulled up a chair.

Speak of the devil.

The south of France suited the cybersecurity expert. His
hair had lightened in the sun, his skin was tanned and he'd
somehow found the time to get a haircut. Frazer ran his hand
over his own skull. He also needed to get a trim before the
wedding, but capturing arms dealers and rescuing little girls
came first.

"*Danke*," Alex said to the woman who delivered his beer.
He turned to them and lowered his voice although he kept a
smile fixed firmly on his lips. He raised his beer in salute. "I'm
gonna drop the *Deutsche* because I happen to know Frazer's
language skills suck."

"I hate speaking German," Killion agreed. "Almost as
much as I hate speaking Russian."

"Maybe they'll send you to Moscow," Frazer suggested
with a hopeful grin.

"Not enough frogs in Moscow," Killion replied. "And too
many fucking Russians."

Speaking of Russians…

"You have your keyring?" Frazer checked. Alex was paranoid about electronic surveillance and always carried a mini signal jammer on his keyring. It came in useful and had stopped a domestic terrorist from blowing up a bunch of people, including Frazer, just a few weeks ago.

Alex let out a breath and some of the tension eased from the tight grasp he had around the neck of his beer bottle. "Yeah, but keep the volume down."

Most of the tables were empty. The waitress behind the bar was noisily restocking mixers.

"When am I going to get one of those things?" Frazer indicated the keyring with a tilt of his head.

"I included one in your best man's gift."

Excellent.

"What about me?" Killion asked.

"Hell, no," Alex replied.

"Why not?"

"You'll share it with Langley," Alex said knowingly.

Killion lowered his forehead into the crook of his elbow, which he'd propped on the table. He laughed. "We're on the same side, you know."

Alex grunted. "I don't want them using my own tools against me. Anyway, they're smart. I'm sure they can figure something out."

Killion wasn't pissed. He liked to wind people up to see what they did. That approach didn't work well on Alex or Frazer. Alex became quiet and Frazer got nasty. It was a miracle they hadn't all killed one another months ago.

"Ashley's working on an ID of the nanny from the image you sent earlier. She make you?" asked Frazer.

Alex shook his head. "I don't think so, but she was staring."

A COLD DARK PROMISE

"Could be your film star good looks," Killion suggested.

Alex grinned. "Naturally. But she's gorgeous. As in supermodel gorgeous and there was something about her eyes. Intelligence."

"Nannies can't be intelligent?" Killion questioned.

"Of course they can be," Alex said patiently. He wasn't taking the bait for an argument. "It was just a certain type of intelligence. I just keep thinking maybe she's working for someone besides Masook." He shrugged in a *what-do-I-know* manner. "Perhaps I'm paranoid."

Frazer raised a brow. No perhaps about that.

"So, you're eyeing the hot nanny and Frazer's kissing another man's woman. You guys are too fast for me." Killion signaled for another beer.

"Saw the kiss. Very convincing," Alex said. "Lucas will kick your ass when he finds out."

"Randall was watching," Killion said with a face full of mischief. "He's probably plotting how to get rid of the body after he kills Frazer in his sleep."

Frazer suppressed the grin that wanted to tug at his lips. "Randall is a professional."

"Exactly." Killion grinned.

"He wasn't happy," Frazer admitted, "but it gives me and Chen good cover and I wanted her here. She's a good agent and skilled at undercover work." He rolled a shoulder. "It's not like I frenched her." He smirked. "I just made it look like I frenched her." He grimaced. "I better tell Izzy before Randall does."

"Pussy," taunted Killion.

"Yeah, I've seen you with Audrey. Makes me want to slap the goofy look off your face."

"Whipped," Killion added, the offending goofy grin firmly in place.

No one would ever accuse Killion of being politically correct.

"Who else is here?" Alex asked.

Frazer was aware they needed to get down to business, although they couldn't make a move until the sun went down. "Matt and Scarlett are honeymooning on a twenty-six-foot sailboat. We also have Noah Zacharias and Logan Masters crewing on the *Ascension*."

Killion leaned in closer. "Logan's had his eye on your Russian friend for a while now. Brits have something on him, and I think they're hoping to use him to flush out his boss."

Alex looked pensive. "I've spotted an Iranian arms buyer and an Israeli. Something tells me this isn't an exchange. It's an auction."

Excitement stirred in Frazer's blood. This provided a unique opportunity to round-up a whole swathe of terrorists and weapons smugglers in one swoop. "Any idea what's being sold?"

Alex pressed his lips together. "Not a clue."

Killion narrowed his gaze. "We could front a buyer."

Alex shook his head. "This deal will happen in the next twenty-four hours and anyone new to the table would spook them—pun intended. No way would these guys hang around in close proximity for any longer than that. Some of them are sworn enemies."

"It's a great way to drive up the price," observed Killion.

"Do you think the weapon is on the boat?" Frazer asked. The CIA knew the illegal arms game better than he did. Serial killers tended to use more hands-on methods of doling out death.

Killion and Alex frowned in unison.

"Not necessarily, but possibly." Alex hedged.

"Why doesn't Ranich sell direct? Why use a broker?"

"It allows him to keep a lower profile and have that degree of separation from terrorists. Plus, he's not the sharpest knife in the drawer." Killion tapped his finger on the tabletop.

"And it's possible Ranich is a buyer, not a seller," added Alex. "I have nothing definitive on that yet."

"And Masook brought his eight-year-old daughter into this nest of serpents?" Not much surprised Frazer anymore.

"Even knowing there's an international warrant out for his arrest. The guy has donkey-sized balls." Killion wiped his lips with the back of his hand.

"That's why Jane thinks local cops might be dirty. It only takes one phone call and he's outta here." Alex's jaw flexed. For all he appeared relaxed on the outside the guy was wound tight. "There's a copter on the boat and another on the Russians'."

"Isn't Masook scared someone might kidnap the kid to make sure they're the ones who get whatever it is he's selling?" Frazer asked. Child kidnapping was something he understood on a personal level and dealt with on a regular basis at work.

"The kidnappers would run the risk of being blacklisted and losing their weapon supply chain. Plus, Masook is just the broker," Alex answered. "The seller might say to hell with the kid."

"Blacklisted from the black-market? Honor amongst terrorists? Why don't they just do the transaction on the dark web?" A couple of tourists strolled in, and Frazer eyed them carefully.

Alex shrugged. "Deals happen there all the time for fire-arms and other ordinance, but they can't be sure the buyer isn't an FBI agent or white-hat hacker who is gonna trace their ass back to base camp. More...*specialized*...items still tend to be sold face-to-face. The players might want to inspect the goods before purchasing, and the seller definitely wants his money transferred before he hands anything over. The different buyers are aware the others all exist but they avoid direct confrontations. I think Masook took the risk with the kid because he's grown cocky and thinks he's invincible. He's either nailing or wants to nail the nanny. Maybe he can't do that in Dubai. Or maybe he just can't live without her?"

They all stared a little morosely into their beers.

"So what's the plan?" asked Alex.

Frazer and the others had discussed the primary course of action on the journey here. "Matt is going to attach listening devices to the hulls of the yachts as soon as it gets dark. Ashley is working on hacking their computers via their Wi-Fi. She's also planning to piggyback on any city surveillance cams and see if we can pick up any other players lurking in the shadows. We need to find out what Masook is selling and round up as many of the people involved as possible."

"What about the local cops?" asked Killion. "You have no powers of arrest here."

"I have the FBI's Legal Attaché to France, and Interpol agents on standby. They agreed to not involve the locals until the last minute to prevent anyone being warned and escaping. The possibility of a weapon turning up on mainland France has them nervous. The French have suffered enough."

Alex picked the label off his beer. He was quiet. Too quiet. Finally he asked, "What about the girl?"

Frazer let a smile curve his lips. "I'm pretty sure that's what you're here for, right?"

"Yep." There was a subtle shift in the atmosphere as Alex relaxed. "Her life probably isn't in immediate danger, which is the only good news about this mess."

"How's Jane Sanders holding up?" Frazer asked.

"Like TNT on a short fuse."

"Where is she?"

"Back at the chateau wearing out the carpet. I have a man watching her."

Killion raised his beer in another toast. "So, all we need to do is rescue the child, identify the players, secure the weapon, and scoop the bad guys up without anyone getting hurt?"

Frazer rolled his shoulders. "And get home in time for the wedding."

"Piece of cake," Killion murmured quietly.

"Let's do it," Alex said. "Let's go stop these bastards."

CHAPTER ELEVEN

M ALLORY TRIED TO let go of the tension that invaded her whole being as she fought rush hour traffic in DC after a long day examining the victims of kidnappers, rapists, and murderers.

"Breathe," she told herself, and felt the phantom of Alex's smile whisper against her skin.

She missed him.

She was pathetic, but she hated him going away like this.

It was wrong of her. She insisted he give her the space do her job, but now that it was his turn to leave her behind she wasn't quite so emphatic about this independence business.

He'd be home soon.

Rex grinned at her in doggy reassurance via the rearview from his position in the backseat. He'd fully recovered from the gunshot wound he'd suffered back in February but, not surprisingly, he didn't like loud noises. He'd come with her to the spa for the weekend, and she'd picked him up from the condo in Quantico before driving back to DC tonight for what she hoped was the last time as a single woman.

"Who's a good boy?"

He panted in happy acknowledgment as he looked out of the window.

There'd been a floral emergency.

Mallory rolled her eyes, grateful she wasn't the sort of person who'd lose it over the color of the flowers in her bouquet. Her mother considered this a minor disaster. Mal didn't give a fig. She'd carry a nosegay of dandelions if necessary, but she was trying to make this wedding perfect for her parents, and they weren't making it easy. First had been the guest list with way too many politicians for Alex's comfort. Then issues over the menu and the cake. They'd added a sponge layer to the cake and a vegetarian option to the menu. It wasn't rocket science. Honestly, Mallory had no clue why people made such a fuss.

It had already been a long day. She and Moira Henderson had been the only ones in the office. Moira had taken advantage of this short window of opportunity to unleash as much spite on Mal as possible in the time she had left before Mallory's leave started.

Mallory had learned to filter out Moira's particular brand of venom, and the woman only revealed her true colors when they were alone, which was rare. Jed Brennan was back in the office tomorrow, and she'd be safe from any overt hostility. You'd think hunting serial killers would be enough ugliness for Moira, but apparently not.

Uncomfortable with sitting for so long with the steering wheel so close to her baby bump she shifted and rubbed her aching back with one hand.

She'd underestimated the amount of work left to do before the wedding, but it was all small details. Maybe she should have taken the whole week off, but she was saving her vacation days for the honeymoon and didn't want to piss off the powers-that-be by taking unpaid leave when she was so close to going on a long maternity leave. She was taking Friday off for a manicure and pedicure and facial treatment with her bridesmaids. The wedding planner should be able to cope with all the other minor details that cropped up.

Seriously. A minister. A groom. Some food and maybe some dancing and she'd be happy. Actually, Alex home safe and she'd be happy.

The baby gave her a sharp kick.

"I'm including you in that thought, junior."

Rex woofed in reply.

They didn't know the sex of the baby and didn't want to know until he or she arrived. The new nursery was neutral in color with yellow walls, pale wooden furniture and white trim.

Mal took a right towards her mother's ridiculously large home.

It was hard to imagine she and Alex would soon be responsible for a child. Alex was installing as much security as a private home could handle—his version of nesting. There had already been a wall around the property. Now electronic lasers and touchpad sensors monitored the grounds and the buildings. The house had a panic room, sprinklers, steel doors, and bulletproof glass in all the windows. It had cost a fortune to install that without sacrificing the character of their Victorian house and that had been her one stipulation. They could live in a fortress, but it had to look like a home.

The upgrades gave Alex something to focus on when he started to worry about what kind of father he'd be. Security was something he could control to a certain point—beyond that no one could control anything. Making these basic precautions allowed him to relax, and she knew he was going to need that cushion when the baby arrived.

She pulled up outside her mother's home and applied the

parking brake. Rex gave another woof. She got out and opened the trunk, grabbed the pile of things her mother had offered to give to the wedding planner on Thursday to bring out to the vineyard on Friday. Mallory could have easily taken them herself, but that would be too easy. Rex took a moment to sniff a lamppost and relieve himself. Mallory was careful on the uneven paving stones. She rang the bell to announce her arrival and then headed straight inside. Even after everything that had happened over the years her mom rarely locked the front door.

Her mother's horrified gasp hit her immediately. "You're not supposed to be carrying anything!"

Mal dumped the packages on the side table in the enormous foyer. "They aren't heavy." She kissed her mother on the cheek and Rex obediently sat, waiting to be noticed. Her mother looked down and gave him a hesitant pat on the top of his golden head.

Mallory studied the senator. Her mom had lost weight since she'd resigned from office last December. The despair that had always pinched her features had lifted some. She looked happier than Mal could ever remember seeing her.

"I picked up all the favors for the groomsmen, maid of honor and bridesmaids," Mallory told her, searching for a neutral topic of conversation.

Her mother shook her head with disapproval. "When I was twenty-seven weeks pregnant I wasn't working full-time and planning a wedding. I was on bed rest."

Mallory touched her mother's arm. "You were having twins, Mom. I'm fine. Honestly." She repeated firmly. "Don't fuss."

Footsteps approached, and Mal looked up to see Art Hanrahan, former head of BAU-4, approaching them warily. Art and her mother were dating and although things were a little strained because of what had happened last year, Mallory liked the guy.

"Can I carry those things into the dining room for you?" he asked.

"Sure." She smiled her thanks. "I told the General"—the wedding planner—"that the color of the anemones wasn't a big deal, and we'd use the ones that had streaks of pink on the edges. And I picked up the candy canes." They'd been specially made with hers and Alex's name shot through them. "She said to remember to put Grandma's cake knife with these other things and she'll pick up everything from here on Thursday night."

Her mother frowned thoughtfully. "Where's Alex?"

In a strange twist of events her mother had become very fond of Mallory's fiancé. Maybe it was guilt.

"Busy at work." No way was she telling them he was away. Her mother would insist on moving in with her, and Mal had spent the last six months trying to repair their relationship. Being pregnant had given her a different perspective on what her parents had gone through when her twin sister, Payton, had been abducted. Even though they'd disagreed on her mother's tactics over the years, Mal wasn't sure she'd have been half as graceful.

Her stomach rumbled, and she rested her hand against her taut belly. "I need to eat before junior starts to do an Alien on me. Would you like to go out to dinner?"

"We were just about to sit down to eat. Join us," Margret insisted. "Cook always makes far too much."

Cook was a French chef who made Mallory's thighs expand an inch every time she walked in the door. What the hell, she'd go swimming tomorrow to make up for it.

"I'll go and set another place," Hanrahan offered cheerily. He held out his hand for Rex's leash and then let him off. Her mother's eyes widened, and she forced herself to look away from where the dog was sniffing the stairs.

"Come on, boy." Hanrahan called him, and Rex darted to follow.

A smile curled her lips as Mallory watched them go. "You two seem cozy."

Her mother's cheeks reddened, and her hands wrung each other. "Art asked me to marry him."

Mal's eyes widened.

Her mother raised her hand and stared at her naked finger. "I said no—for now. I didn't want to steal the limelight on your big day."

Mallory shook her head slowly from side to side and took her mother's hands in hers. "That's not how Alex and I roll. The more good news the better. Do you love him?" she asked softly.

Her mother gave a self-conscious laugh and looked away. "I do. After your father, I didn't expect to ever fall in love again but…"

Tears filled Mallory's eyes. Man, she couldn't wait for the pregnancy hormones to be over. "I'll leave you two to have a nice romantic dinner and you tell him yes—"

"No." Her mother held on to her hands tighter. "I want to see you put your feet up, and I want to see you eat. I'll tell Art that I changed my mind when we're alone together…later."

Mallory's brows stretched high.

"What?" her mother queried. "You think old people don't

have sex?"

Mallory choked out a laugh. "One, you're not old. Two, no one wants to think of their parents getting it on with someone. Seriously."

Margret's answering smile was soft. "I know. I love you, Mallory. I never said it enough after we lost Payton. It was like I lost everything good in my heart, and I became a bitter and hateful woman." She looked away and swallowed hard. "I died that day. There are no words or deeds that can take away a parent's guilt in that situation. Every day I berated myself for keeping you girls in a bedroom so far away from mine, for not having fifty guard dogs and an alarm system and bodyguards. When I wasn't blaming myself, I was blaming your father." Her lips firmed, but she kept going. "And you."

The honesty was as shocking as it was refreshing.

Her mother's fingers squeezed until it was almost painful. "I'm sorry. I'm sorry I wasn't a better person. I'm sorry I wasn't the sort of mother you deserved especially after you lost your sister. I failed you terribly. I should have been stronger for the ones left behind."

Now Mallory was flat out crying as she pulled her mother into an embrace. "It was a terrible time. I can't imagine what you went through. I love you, Mom. You and Dad. I love you both. I want you both to be happy."

After a few minutes her mother pulled away and wiped a finger under each eye. "That's all I want for you, too."

Mallory coaxed her mother into the smaller eating area inside the kitchen, rather than the huge formal dining room. And as she started to eat she sent up a little prayer that Alex was safe. She understood her mom so much better nowadays, and life was too short to hang onto old grievances. This wedding was exactly what her parents needed to focus on the future and let go of the past. Alex was all that Mallory needed. He was all she'd ever need.

CHAPTER TWELVE

A S SOON AS it got dark the team set up a command center at the chateau while Alex pushed thoughts of Mallory and their upcoming wedding to the back of his mind. He needed to concentrate on the mission if he was going to retrieve Taylor safely.

He and Ashley Chen were in the process of hooking up computers to the listening devices Matt Lazlo had attached to each of the larger boats in the marina earlier that evening. They both wore headphones and suddenly Ashley gave a huge smile. It wasn't that long ago neither one of them had trusted the other, now she was in the wedding party.

She unplugged the headset so everyone could hear. Everyone quieted down. This feed was from Masook's boat.

Tinny, indistinct voices came over the speakers. Ashley enhanced the feed as much as she could, boosted the volume, and suddenly a female voice piped up something in English about going horse riding the next day.

Alex glanced to where Jane hovered uncertainly near the door, watching everyone with a mixture of hope and trepidation. At the girl's voice Jane put her hand over her mouth and appeared to hold back a sob.

What would it feel like to hear your child's voice after four long years of silence? Heart-wrenching, and not nearly enough.

Jane knew all these people wouldn't all be here if it were a simple extraction, and yet, she'd said nothing. She wasn't a stupid woman. She was a desperate mother. He exchanged a look with Reilly who acknowledged him almost imperceptibly.

They couldn't afford for Jane to fuck up this op by being too emotionally invested in the outcome and doing something rash.

"Listen." Ashley grabbed his sleeve and tugged him down beside her. She'd filtered and refined the audio further. It was even clearer now.

"*It's safe?*" An unknown speaker asked. The voice was muffled.

"*As long as no one opens the containers, it's safe.*"

Every person in the room froze and looked at one another. What the hell was in the containers?

"Is that Masook?" Alex asked Jane. Her eyes had gone huge with horror. She nodded.

"*That's the antidote?*" asked the first man.

Something about the other voice in the room niggled at Alex's memory, but he couldn't place it.

"*The vaccine. Yes.*"

Well, shit. Vaccine suggested biological. He exchanged a look with Frazer.

"*There doesn't seem to be very much of it.*" The voice held a trace of irony.

"Who is that?" Alex demanded. Sound quality was poor. "Anyone got an image or an ID?" They'd been photographing everyone going on and off the boat.

"*My supplier is working on making more.*"

"*How do I know it's real?*"

There was a laugh. *"Have I ever let you down in the past?"*

There was a jumbled confusion of words as several different conversations were picked up at the same time. Ashley bent to try and zero in on Masook. Alex checked the camera feed and sure enough a group of well-dressed people were coming onboard the boat—presumably for drinks or dinner.

"Can you isolate Masook and the buyer?" he asked Ashley.

She pulled a face. "I'm not sure. This isn't my expertise."

Alex nodded. "Mine either. We can untangle it later." Everything was being recorded. But they might miss something vital in the meantime.

"We could get Scarlett in here…" Ashley looked at Frazer. "She'd be better at this than any of us."

Frazer said nothing for a moment. Matt and Scarlett weren't supposed to get any more involved than they already were.

Masook's voice suddenly came through, as clearly as if he were standing beside the listening device. *"Tell the captain we set sail on the morning tide."*

"He's leaving?" asked Jane in a panicked voice while taking a step forward.

Alex exchanged a glance with Frazer. "Can we get an ID on the buyer? Is he taking anything with him? Because if he is we need to grab him now, before he disappears with whatever the hell Masook is trying to sell."

"Noah's on it," said Logan, talking into his cell. Noah and Lucas were back on Greenburg's boat, *Ascension*, watching the live surveillance feed and keeping a close eye on their prey.

A door banged on the boat.

"We're leaving? You promised Taylor she could go riding tomorrow. What should I tell her?" Josette's voice came

through the speakers. She sounded a little breathless.

"Tell her I'll buy her a pony when we get home. After this trip, I can buy her an entire stable if she wishes. But I didn't come here to talk about Taylor." Masook's voice grew low and husky.

Josette laughed. *"But your dinner guests just arrived."*

"They can wait. I can't."

There was a bump and indistinct rustle of material being moved aside and heavy breathing. Then grunting as two people had fast, rough sex against thin cabin walls.

"I guess that answers the question about the nanny." Killion grimaced.

Alex glanced at Frazer. "Sounds like he's celebrating a sale."

"What about Taylor?" Jane demanded loudly.

Alex held her gaze. "We'll get her back." But things had become a lot more complicated. A lot more dangerous.

"Here's an image of the person we believe Masook was just talking to," Logan interrupted. "Noah says he's now on deck with the other dinner guests *sans* biological weapon unless it's small enough to fit in his jacket pocket, which it could be. He'll try to get a better shot. I'm sending the first picture to your cells." Logan pressed a button.

Alex downloaded it onto his phone. Despite the shadows, Noah had managed to isolate an image of a swarthy, good-looking guy with a sharp nose and an elegant demeanor. He wore a hat and sunglasses even in the gloom—effective at fooling facial recognition programs, but not humans.

Alex never forgot a face.

Hatred rose inside him like smoke and bile. Charles Salamander. The guy Alex had been ordered to assassinate by the

US government years ago. Unfortunately, Alex had frozen when the man's young daughter had walked into the room, and he couldn't go through with it. Alex had been captured and imprisoned, the US government cutting ties and denying any association. Salamander had extracted some excruciating personal revenge in that Moroccan jail, revenge Alex still wore on his skin today.

No one here knew of the connection between Alex and Salamander though Killion had also recognized the man's face and was cursing.

"That motherfucker is bad news. Interpol has issued several Red Notices for his arrest."

"So, there are at least four people in Antibes tonight who have active warrants out on them. Whatever is in those canisters has a lot of people taking some serious risks," mulled Frazer.

"Are we assuming the supplier is Ranich?" Logan put in.

Alex slowly shook his head. "If it's a new biological Ranich could as easily be a buyer as a seller. We need to take a look at Masook's computer. We need to figure out who is supplying this stuff to Masook."

"We need to know what it is," Frazer added.

And they needed to know now. Before that canister disappeared.

"We don't have the manpower or authority to arrest all these people without spooking the others," said Alex. They had five FBI agents on the ground, but none of them had powers of arrest in a foreign country.

"I'll talk to Interpol," said Frazer. "As long as they know where the bad guys are they can grab them using local cops when we tell them to. They can take the credit. This will be a big scoop for them and they could do with some good publicity when it comes to crushing terrorists."

"We need to spring this simultaneously, and we'll need eyes on each of the players," said Frazer. "Killion watch Salamander. Lucas can take the Indian contingent, Logan the Hezbollah representative, Noah can monitor the Russians from *Ascension*, Matt the Israelis. I'll follow the Al Qaeda contact. Alex takes Masook."

Alex shook his head. "I'll need Matt in a boat. Let's get Scarlett up here and she and Ashley can run comms and keep up the remote surveillance to warn us of any unexpected developments," he said. "We can't watch everyone, but if we monitor critical points we should be able to spot most of the players if they try to leave Antibes. I go in first. As soon as I have the weapon in hand, the kid, and Masook's computer, you give Interpol the word to go. Everyone rendezvous on *Ascension* when we are done."

"How are you going to achieve all that without Masook seeing you?" Frazer asked sardonically.

Alex looked at Jane. "Easy. We're going to create a diversion. Jane's going to help." He watched her face turn ashen, and she swayed slightly.

He was asking her to face her greatest fear.

Reilly stepped forward, wearing a dark frown. "How *exactly* is Jane going to cause a distraction?"

"She just has to make a scene," Alex said.

"I don't like that plan," said Reilly.

"Why not?" asked Alex.

"I've spent the last few days keeping her away from that asshole," Reilly said bluntly.

It was one of the things Alex liked about him. Jack Reilly

was a no bullshit kind of guy.

"Masook isn't going to harm Jane in front of witnesses, and she's going to stay firmly on the quay and not get on the boat. While Masook is looking at her, and likely panicking if he hasn't made the exchange of the bioweapon for money yet, I'm going to be below deck, grabbing the bioweapon and computer, which I'll pass over the side to Matt who is going to immediately bring them back here. As soon as they are off the boat I'll grab Taylor."

"She's not going to go willingly," Jane warned. Alex watched her as her teeth started to chatter. She was genuinely terrified, and he wished there was another way. He couldn't think of one that wouldn't leave the weapon or the kid vulnerable.

"I won't hurt Taylor, but I'm not drugging a child," said Alex. But he might scare her. There was no way to prevent that.

"What's to stop Masook from dragging Jane onboard and beating the crap out of her?" Reilly asked with his arms crossed over his chest.

Alex blinked. Reilly had never balked at a plan before. Then Alex got it. The usually professional, unflappable bodyguard had developed feelings for Jane. But Alex's plan wouldn't put her in real jeopardy. As long as everyone did their job she'd be fine.

"You are. Pretend to be a tourist taking a walk. Step in if Masook turns threatening."

Jane exchanged a look with Reilly and Alex noticed her expression soften when she took in the former Green Beret.

As a man due to get married in a few days' time, Alex wasn't about to get in the way of a budding romance, but he also didn't want to fuck up this op. There were too many people he cared about involved, in addition to the presence of an unspecified bioweapon and a child.

He checked his watch. "Wheels up in thirty minutes. Frazer, talk to Matt and tell him what's going down. Get Scarlett up here pronto. Everyone else, gear up."

"Aye aye, Captain," Frazer said cheerfully.

"Ashley. I want every piece of information we can get on the whereabouts of each of these players. Let's see if we can use street cameras for real time surveillance and track cell phones to fix locations until we get eyes-on. Can we talk to Langley and get some additional resources on this?"

Killion nodded and started dialing. "I'll ask."

Alex checked his weapon.

Frazer threw him a flak-jacket. "Put that on."

Alex made a face.

"I need to get you to the altar without any missing pieces or 9mm body piercings. Everyone wears body armor," Frazer said loudly. "French police will step in to make the arrests. As soon as Alex gets the weapon and girl off the boat Interpol calls in the cops. Even if Masook is warned at that point he can do very little about it, except run." Frazer eyed Alex. "Perhaps it would be an idea to stop by the helicopter and make sure it can't take off?"

"What about the Russian's machine?" Ashley asked.

"Pilot just went to refuel," Logan said. "Think Interpol could figure out an excuse to make sure the roundtrip lasts longer than necessary?"

Frazer nodded. "I'll call my contact."

"That contact better be solidly on our side," warned Alex. Just call him cynical, but he'd been in the business long enough not to trust any unknown factors.

"I guess we'll find out," Frazer said cryptically.

"Here goes nothing." Alex stood. As much as he wanted to call Mallory he didn't. He needed to focus on the mission.

CHAPTER THIRTEEN

J ANE'S HANDS SHOOK as she pulled off the pale-blue t-shirt she'd been wearing and reached for a long-sleeve, black t-shirt Ashley Chen had lent her. As excited as she was at the thought of seeing Taylor again, she was also terrified. Of Ahmed. Of the possibility Taylor would reject her, and she'd be forced to drag a screaming child away from the only parent she knew. No way in hell was Jane leaving Taylor with a man who trafficked weapons and indiscriminate death. Jane took a couple of deep breaths, fighting panic, trying to steady herself.

There was a rap on the door and, without waiting for an answer, Jack Reilly strode in, then stopped short. Ignoring the fact she was in her underwear, he closed the door quietly behind him. He held a plate with a sandwich on it.

"Are you okay?" he asked.

She nodded, her insides a mix of anticipation, sickly trepidation and downright fear. She was such a coward.

"You need to eat." There was the ever-present glass of water, which he held out to her.

Her throat felt like sandpaper, but she couldn't face eating or drinking anything. She turned away. "I can't."

She awkwardly pulled the t-shirt over her head. The material was tight and clingy, and she was apparently larger than Ashley Chen in the chest department. It felt more like a compression bandage than an item of clothing. Jane rolled the stretchy fabric down over her sports bra and looked up, surprised to find Jack's eyes on her body with a glint in their depths that was far from clinical or professional.

They'd spent a lot of time together over the last few days, and she'd enjoyed it more than she'd expected. Since he'd rejected her sexual overtures they'd just hung out. But, right now, his eyes told her he wasn't indifferent to her as a woman. Which meant he'd been telling the truth—he didn't mix business with pleasure.

Pity.

Now it was too late. After they got back to the States she doubted she'd see him again.

She stepped into a pair of her own black pants and zipped up. Sitting on the edge of the bed she pulled on black socks then black boots. She looked like a cat burglar, or one of the operatives outside.

"This is not what I wear. He'll know something is up if I turn up dressed like Cat Woman." She shook her head, disgusted with herself, and dragged the top off. She stalked to her suitcase and started rooting through her clothes.

She found a dark blue jersey dress with a beaded neckline. Her back to Reilly, she dragged off her bra and tossed it aside for a strapless one. She put the bra on, aware of Reilly's gaze on her back though she didn't turn around. This wasn't a seduction and even if it was, she knew it wouldn't work on this man. She was his *client*. She pulled the dress over her head, and the material draped softly over her body. She'd always liked this dress because it flattered her curves, making her waist look smaller. She kicked off her boots and dragged her pants down her legs, tossing them in the suitcase.

"Nice socks." Reilly's voice was low, and vibrated with more than just amusement. She glanced over her shoulder in surprise.

His jaw was clenched, and his nostrils flared.

She raised her brows. "Regretting all that time we wasted playing Crazy Eights?" she teased.

"Getting to know you wasn't wasted time."

She blinked. The guy was always thoughtful about the things he said. If he was trying to seduce her mind he was going the right way about it.

He drew in a deep breath, and his lips twitched. "But I'm wishing I'd thrown in a few rounds of strip poker to shake things up a little."

She laughed as she bent over and pulled off her socks, tossing them in the case, too. "Not sure I would have been able to keep my hands to myself if you were naked, Mr. Reilly, and I seem to remember you didn't like me touching you."

"I'd like it just fine if I wasn't at work. What I don't like is being treated like a piece of meat."

Her mouth dropped open in horror. "Oh, my goodness. That is not what I was thinking when I touched you the other day."

"What, then?" he demanded.

Her eyes widened as she took in his disbelieving expression. She swallowed. "I was trying to get rid of you."

"Seriously?" He sounded dubious.

She nodded. "That's how it started out." She retrieved a pair of low-heeled sandals and slid them onto her feet. She met his gaze. "But after I touched you I would happily have taken a few hours of sexual oblivion."

His brow quirked. "Oblivion? Where's the fun in that? I'd

want to remember every detail."

Her heart suddenly pounded. God, yes. She definitely wanted to have sex with this man one day.

"You need to eat and drink so you have energy to complete the op," Reilly told her, sliding quickly back into the role of chief guardian.

Her mouth curved. "You make it sound like I'm about to compete in hand-to-hand combat." She flinched at her own words.

That was the terrible truth about having someone you loved beat the ever-loving crap out of you. The memory could hit just as hard as the punches.

The pity in Reilly's bright blue eyes proved what she'd already suspected. Either he'd overheard her conversation with Alex the other day or Alex had filled him in on her abuse.

She sat on the bed, hating that her secrets had been revealed. She didn't want this man's pity. She didn't want anyone's pity. "Don't," she said, tersely.

He came around and sat beside her. Bumped her shoulder like they were a couple of teens. "Don't what?"

She huffed out a reluctant laugh. "Feel sorry for me."

"I don't feel sorry for you. I'm in awe you had the guts to leave him. That must have been terrifying. And I'm in awe you're willing to face him again tonight."

"It's for my daughter. I'd do anything for her. I'd die to protect her." Her hands tightened back into fists.

"It's not going to come to that." He held her gaze. "I won't let it get that far."

She'd attended support groups for battered women and it had helped. She knew the cycle of violence was about power and control and not about love. But deep down she always harbored a little blame—she was the one who'd been foolish enough to fall in love with an abuser. "It was my own fault. I made a bad choice."

He thrust the plate into her one hand and the water into the other. "You fell in love with a man who didn't deserve you. But he's the one who made the decision to hit you. It's on him. Always on him."

She took a bite of the soft bread. Salt from the butter and succulent cured ham hit her tongue and she realized she was starving.

"He didn't deserve you."

She glanced up at Reilly's face, stunned to realize he seemed to genuinely care about her. It had been so long since she'd allowed anyone to get close, to see her weaknesses.

"Eat," he told her.

She bit into her sandwich. She needed fuel. She hadn't eaten since all these people had arrived at the chateau and it had become clear Alex hadn't told her the truth about what was going on. She'd tried to be angry with him, but had put herself in his shoes. He'd had to choose between saving one child versus containing a bioweapon.

It was a no-brainer, except when that child was yours.

"Did you know what was going on with Ahmed? About him being a suspected arms dealer?" she asked Reilly. Was she the only one who'd been kept ignorant?

Faint lines creased the corner of his eyes as he frowned, but there was an honesty in his gaze that made her breath catch.

"No, I didn't. I don't think Alex expected the cavalry to turn up like this today, either. My assignment was to look out for you, which is why I hate the idea of you confronting your ex now."

She flinched. The idea of being just a job hurt.

"Hey," he said, reading her correctly. "Didn't mean I didn't enjoy being your protection." He moved a tendril of hair across her cheek and behind her ear. She shivered, and he mistook her reaction for fear. "Not all men are scumbags, you know."

"I do know." She hunched her shoulders and took another bite of her sandwich, wishing she didn't have these tangled feelings for her bodyguard. How clichéd could she be? How pathetically desperate and needy to be attracted to this guy.

"I still feel like an idiot for marrying Ahmed and I don't trust myself now not to make another colossal mistake."

He pressed his lips together, and she couldn't help but imagine them on her skin.

"How about when this is all over I teach you some basic self-defense moves? That way if you do 'make a mistake,'" his voice roughened with what might have been disapproval, but she didn't think it was aimed at her, "you can at least try to fight back."

She took a sip of water. Wiped her mouth with the back of her trembling hand. Her eyes met and held his. "I doubt I'll see you again once this is over."

"What if you did?" She read more than professional interest in his gaze now. "What do you have to lose if all I do is teach you how to make someone hurt so bad they can't even scream?"

What would it hurt? Nothing, she realized. It would feel good to know how to fight back. It was about time she built something constructive out of her fear. The real risk was spending more time with Reilly—taking a chance on being someone's friend was much scarier than taking a lover.

If she had Taylor back, being able to defend herself and her child would be a good thing. If she didn't...she forced that thought out of her mind.

"I'd like that." She looked down and realized that although she'd thought she couldn't eat a bite, she'd actually polished off the whole sandwich and most of the water. He'd got her to think about something besides confronting her ex and finding her daughter. She smiled slightly.

"That's settled then," he said. As if the future was guaranteed.

And the idea of seeing him again after this was all over...she didn't like how excited that made her feel. Like a teen catching sight of her crush.

"Thank you." She touched his hand, and he stilled for a moment. "For everything."

Reilly took the plate and cup from her and stood. She found herself looking up his flat stomach and broad chest, all the way to those calm, intelligent eyes that were the same blue as the Aegean Sea. He reached out and slid his hand gently along her jawline. One side of his wide mouth kicked up. "Let's go get your kid back."

CHAPTER FOURTEEN

D RESSED ALL IN black and carrying a waterproof sack on his back, Alex soundlessly climbed the rope up the side of the *Fair Winds* and slid over the rail onto the deck. Tinkling laughter came from the stern where Masook and his guests sat enjoying nightcaps. Intel on the other guests suggested they were potential investors in Masook's legitimate construction business that the Saudi was trying to expand, probably as part of his cover for being here. They appeared innocent regarding Masook's illegal arms dealing—on the surface, anyway.

All except Salamander.

The fact Alex wanted to put a bullet between Salamander's too-close-together eyes was beside the point. Salamander's death wasn't his objective today, and Alex had plenty of experience compartmentalizing his emotions.

Whatever Masook was selling must be worth a lot of money if Charles Salamander had dared to risk leaving Morocco.

Alex paused in the shadows and glanced toward the *Ascension.* Noah Zacharias was keeping watch on both Alex and the Russians. The man sent a click to Alex's PTT headset to indicate the coast was clear.

There were two guards on each deck. Alex headed up a ladder to where the helicopter crouched like a big, fat hornet. First, he took out the guard at the prow, dragging the unconscious man out of sight, binding him, and removing the guard's earpiece and inserting it into his own ear. Alex dropped the guard's gun quietly into the water and headed back toward the copter.

The second guard stood watching the quay. Alex waited until the sentry moved out of sight of the Russian vessel moored on the other side of the *Fair Winds*. Alex didn't doubt the Russians would be watching this boat to keep an eye on the biological weapon, and to gather any potential *Kompromat* on people aboard. Alex had no desire to appear on their radar.

He put the guard in a sleeper hold. Then zip-tied his wrists and ankles together, slapping duct-tape over the man's mouth. Alex removed comms and weapons before quietly dropping them into the water with a silent apology to the fish.

They'd discussed the best way to disable the helicopter and had gone with Logan Masters's suggestion, which Alex attached carefully to the tail rotor, before setting the detonator. He wished he could be a little more blasé about using explosives.

He shrugged out of the light-weight, black, zippered jacket, revealing a white shirt, black bow tie and cufflinks. He wore black dress pants and pulled black dress shoes out of his bag and slipped them on his bare feet. He'd borrowed the clothes from Frazer who'd obviously been channeling James Bond when he'd packed for this mission.

"Heading down." He barely moved his lips, but it would be enough for Ashley Chen and Scarlett Stone who manned the communication network to hear. They'd found a blueprint of the boat on the computers of the original designers. The biggest danger was bumping into staff or security below decks, but they'd decided with dinner guests onboard, hiding in plain sight would be more effective than creeping around the place. Blending in was one of the things Alex excelled at, right up until the point he pulled out his weapon and pulled the trigger.

He could hear the group laughing and joking in French on the deck below.

Salamander's gleeful smile as he raised a knife teased Alex's memory, but he pushed it aside. He didn't plan on killing anyone today, but he would secure the weapon, and the child, using whatever means necessary.

He headed inside and down the carpeted corridor. Down another deck, and another, until he hit the region where heat signatures suggested Masook was keeping the weapon.

The idea of biologicals made his skin literally crawl. Who did that? Released something that would target innocent civilians as well as military operatives? And who knew how these biologicals would behave once they reached the general population—how they'd morph and spread. Warfare was often unethical and illegal. Covert ops even more so. But Alex had his own ideals—ideals he wouldn't compromise. The use of biological or chemical weapons crossed a line he would never condone and would do everything to stop.

Alex tried the door of the room where they'd assumed the weapon was being stored. An office Masook was using. The door was locked, but it took only a few seconds to open. He closed the door carefully behind him as Noah confirmed in his ear all was quiet on deck.

Alex began a systematic search of the room using the light that streamed through the porthole. He couldn't risk a flashlight, but he didn't need one. A laptop computer sat on Masook's desk.

Alex thought about the conversation he'd overheard between Salamander and Masook. Where would Masook have hidden the material onboard a boat like this—a boat where his eight-year-old daughter was staying?

Alex glanced around the room and moved aside a beautiful abstract painting of a seascape. Sure enough, a sleek black electronic safe stared right back at him.

He smiled.

CHAPTER FIFTEEN

T HE HARBOR WAS pretty at night, Jane realized as she walked toward the quay. Lights from the ancient fortress, nearby houses and the multitude of boats reflected in the calm water, creating a scene worthy of a picture postcard. The scent of French cooking hung redolent on the air, the sounds of people talking and laughing trickled over old stone, reassuringly normal in a world that had been turned upside down by what she now knew lurked onboard her ex-husband's boat.

A cool breeze brushed over her, and she shivered. She wasn't wearing a flak jacket. She'd refused pointblank even when Lincoln Frazer had gone all FBI *I'm-the-boss-of-you* on her. Alex had already left by that point otherwise she might have caved. But she was the one person Ahmed might physically grab tonight and she refused to jeopardize the operation by wearing a bulletproof vest.

She could take a punch.

She'd proved it on more than one occasion, but she would not be the one who screwed this thing up. She had too much to lose.

For the first time ever, she was part of a team of people who were not only trying to help get her baby back, but were also going after arms dealers and killers.

It made her feel proud. And terrified.

Her work in The Gateway Project had felt justified at the time. The difference was, this operation had Interpol in the background bringing these bad guys legally to justice. The Gateway Project had acted as judge, jury, and executioner. They'd been wrong, but she didn't regret removing pedophiles and serial killers from the streets. Too many innocents had died at their hands.

But they'd still been wrong, and she was just as guilty as Alex. At least he'd had the honesty to pull the trigger, not just provide information and deceive herself that her hands had no blood on them.

She had blood on them. Gallons and gallons of the stuff.

Her low heels hit the quay and her footsteps rang like a death knell. She could just make out the massive boats in the distance and forced her pace not to falter. She passed luxury liners and fast cars, women wearing *Prada* and men in *Versace*. Once this had been her world, but for all its sparkle and glamor it was a cold and lonely place.

She rolled her shoulders and wondered where Reilly was. Presumably up ahead on the pier.

There was something about the way he looked at her that made her quiver. It wasn't just lust, it wasn't just pity, it wasn't disinterest. It was...*interest*. He was interested in who she was.

When was the last time *that* had happened?

He'd offered to teach her self-defense...

The idea was tantalizing on so many levels she couldn't let herself think about it. She knew how to shoot a gun, but the idea of grappling with a man and knowing how to prevent him from hurting her, how to hurt him back...she wanted that. She *really* wanted that. And the idea of Jack Reilly getting all hot and sweaty while teaching her? She wanted that, too. But first, she needed to concentrate on the most important thing in her life.

Taylor.

The boat Ahmed was staying on was just up ahead now. Did the man he'd borrowed it from know about Ahmed's business sideline? She had a feeling the NSA and CIA would be trying to figure that out in the near future.

Beautiful people in expensive clothes were standing on the gangplank, which led from the yacht to the quay. Shiny, expensive cars were parked next to the sea wall. The dinner party must be breaking up. She needed to move fast if she wanted witnesses.

She wasn't wearing a headset because if she was captured their team didn't want Ahmed's people to know she had help. She was the distraction. She didn't intend to be the weak link.

And there he was. A man she'd once loved with all her heart. A man whose child she'd born. A man who had beaten her more times than she could count. He was still rugged and handsome. Well groomed. Sharp-eyed. Intelligent. Violent. Mean. Small minded. Vicious.

Her lungs squeezed as hatred and fear nearly overwhelmed her.

If it hadn't been for Taylor she'd have shot the bastard years ago and to hell with it. But Jane didn't want that to be her legacy. She wanted to be a good person. A good mother. She needed to regain the self-worth he'd stripped from her.

When she was twenty yards from the boat, Ahmed looked up and away from his guests and his gaze found her, unerringly. He'd always been able to sense her presence. His back straightened. Surprise flickered over his face, replaced by satisfaction, then anger and alarm.

He spoke into a radio that was attached to his cuff, and she saw shadows move on the deck.

Ahmed's guests seemed to sense the sudden tension in the air and started to move toward their waiting sports cars. The women would kill themselves trying to walk down these old, cobbled streets in their skyscraper heels.

Ahmed clearly wanted to wait for his guests to leave before confronting her, but that wouldn't be making a scene now, would it?

"Hello, Ahmed. I want to see our child." She spoke clearly and calmly, and her voice echoed powerfully across the water.

"Who is this, Ahmed?" a tall man with a French accent asked him.

"No one. A crazy person." Ahmed moved down the gangplank and tried to hurry the man toward his Porsche.

"I must have been crazy to marry you, and believe your lies," Jane continued calmly. It helped to see Jack Reilly meandering slowly along the quay toward them.

"This is your wife?" another man asked.

"Ex," Ahmed said bitterly.

Oh, he still hated her for divorcing him.

"I thought you said she was dead, *mon ami*?"

Jane smiled coldly. "If had been up to him, I would be."

"What does she mean?" the tall man demanded.

"Nothing. She is a nasty woman who tried to steal from me—"

"You stole from me the only thing that matters. Our child. There is an Interpol Red Notice out for your arrest, and I demand you hand her over to me."

The guests looked a little startled at that.

Jane raised the volume but kept her voice calm. No one

ever listened to hysterical women. "I want my child back. If you don't hand her over as per the court order, I am going to call the police."

"She isn't here." Ahmed looked flustered now. Torn between not looking like an ass in front of potential investors and probably wanting to kill her with his bare hands, and worried his secret arms deal was going to spiral down the toilet thanks to her actions.

She hoped so.

The guests looked at one another. One couple hurried to their car, clearly uncomfortable with confrontation. She'd been like that once. Scared. Pitiful. The other two couples hovered nearby, unsure what to do.

"Perhaps you two need to talk about this amicably," the Frenchman tried. "It is surely better for the child to try and work together like mature adults than to argue?"

Jane cocked her head. "I haven't seen my daughter for four years because I was stupid enough to think Ahmed would act like a mature adult. He abducted her on her first court appointed visitation."

"Not true!"

Two of Ahmed's henchmen moved down the gangplank. Good. If they were watching her, they weren't likely to bump into Alex.

"Of course, that was after he spent three years of marriage beating the hell out of me every opportunity he got."

One of Ahmed's goons grabbed her by her upper arm. "Time to move along."

"Bring her onboard," Ahmed bit out.

She pried the guard's fingers from her arm. "So, you can beat me again? Maybe kill me this time and dump my body in the Med?"

"Hey!" The voice was very male and American. Dear and familiar. It had soothed her repeatedly over the last few interminable days. "You need some help, ma'am?"

Reilly.

She could easily fall in love with a man like Jack Reilly.

The boat's engines started, and everyone looked around in confusion. Ahmed darted back onto the ship, shouting in Arabic. The smell of diesel smoke filled the air. She noticed someone preparing to cast off and started to panic. This wasn't part of the plan. One man tried to drag her toward the gangplank but Reilly smashed him in the face. The tall Frenchman shouted at the other goon who looked like he was about to grab her. Instead they both let her go and sprinted up the gangplank, then pulled it aboard. The boat started to pull away from the sea wall.

Reilly wrapped his arms around her, holding her in place while she sobbed. "What about Taylor? What about—"

He pressed her face into his chest, smothering what she was about to say.

She gripped his t-shirt. Tears filled her eyes as despair bloomed inside. "I'm never going to see my baby again, am I?"

Reilly drew in a big breath and spoke quietly into her ear. "You have to trust Alex Parker to get the job done. He'll protect Taylor. He'll get her back for you."

She wouldn't be bowed, but she just wasn't sure if she believed in miracles anymore. She lifted her chin and nodded as she watched the boat motor away.

Another question was, who was going to protect Alex? The odds were impossible now the former assassin had been cut off from his backup. Guilt rose up inside her. She'd dragged him into this mess when he'd been trying so hard to escape and live a normal life. How would she ever live with herself if anything happened to him? How would she ever face Mallory Rooney if she got him killed?

CHAPTER SIXTEEN

F RAZER WAS IN a strip joint in the seedier side of the French Riviera. Two suspected Al Qaeda members were sitting front and center of the runway while another wannabe jihadist was using the can. Frazer couldn't feign interest in the naked women on stage so he watched with a bored, cynical air that fit right in. It was clear that the women in this club didn't enjoy their jobs. But then, Frazer knew many were trafficked, others were junkies, most needed the money to feed their families.

Hard to get aroused by exploitation and desperation.

His cell rang. Chen. "Masook hauled ass out of the harbor as soon as he saw Jane. Alex is still onboard with Masook and the Moroccan. Killion is hightailing it to *Ascension* to follow them."

Frazer swore. This was not good news, but they couldn't abandon their plan. Alex could take care of himself, and the kid. Hopefully. Even as Frazer thought it dread sliced through him. If anything happened to the guy Frazer would never forgive himself.

More importantly, Mal would never forgive him.

"Okay. Let's bring Interpol in on the players we have under surveillance." These terrorists needed to be stopped.

There were a few seconds pause as Chen called their liaison, then, "Done. They're splitting into teams. ETA ten minutes. Logan, Noah and Killion are now all on the *Ascension*. Should they keep watching the Russian's boat or follow Masook?"

He needed to be on that vessel before it left port.

"Send Matt to follow Masook. He'll be less obtrusive. I'm on my way to the boat and will be there just as soon as I can. Can you get a visual on Alex's cell?"

Chen laughed despite the strain. "For once, yes. I see him."

"Whatever happens, don't lose that boat."

"Aye aye, Captain."

The third Al Qaeda suspect came back into view with a smile on his face. Frazer suspected he'd had a private lap dance in one of the backrooms. One of the other men climbed to his feet and headed in the same direction.

Frazer checked his watch. These guys were going to be preoccupied for a little while and, even if they weren't, he needed to help Alex. He slipped outside into the fresh air and saw the first stirring of police activity at the far end of the ally. As much as he wanted to stay and watch the show he had bigger concerns. If Alex had only been dealing with Masook Frazer wouldn't be worried, but the Moroccan, Charles Salamander, had an evil reputation.

Frazer hurried back toward the main street and hailed a cab. The shit and the fan had just collided at high speed.

CHAPTER SEVENTEEN

A LEX HAD JUST opened the safe when he heard the engines start.

"Masook is on the move. Jane is safely on the quay with Reilly." The words came through his earpiece, courtesy of Noah.

Shit.

Inside the safe was a bright red, waterproof case. Alex retrieved it and carefully opened the lid.

Five, small, glass vials were nestled alongside an array of hypodermics and surgical gloves. Four vials were filled with powder the color of bleached bone and labeled *Bacillus anthracis*.

Alex frowned. Anthrax?

Presumably the fifth vial of liquid was the vaccine.

Alex had received anthrax vaccinations during his military service, and yearly boosters while working for the CIA. He hadn't had an injection in a few years but he should have some immunity left over, which may or may not keep him alive if he was exposed. Not that he wanted to test that hypothesis.

As deadly as anthrax undoubtedly was—a Category A biological agent, posing the highest potential risk—it didn't make sense for this many buyers to be vying for this particular organism of death, considering so many countries had their own biological weapons programs. Unless it had been weaponized in some way…

Great.

Through the guard's stolen headphones Alex could hear a commotion going on. He quickly snapped closed the bright red, waterproof box and shut the safe, replacing the painting that hid it. He picked up Masook's laptop, placed it inside two, large, sealable, plastic bags. He stuffed the whole thing into a laptop bag that sat on the floor and attached a glow stick to the strap. The hard, waterproof case wouldn't fit inside the laptop bag's zip pocket so he attached it via the strap and slung the whole thing over his back. He pulled his SIG Sauer with his right hand and headed to the door.

If he could toss the anthrax and the laptop over the side, Matt could retrieve it from the water. Then Alex would grab the kid and swim them both to shore. The French authorities could pick up Masook and anyone else involved from the boat at their convenience. And at their own peril. Alex had a wedding to attend. He pushed Charles Salamander out of his head. He had better things to think about than revenge.

Maybe he wasn't quite as black inside as he sometimes feared.

He slipped out of the office but heard footsteps coming down the stairs at the end of the corridor. He ducked into a dark cabin that was thankfully empty and listened at the door. There was a lot of jabbering in Arabic in his ear from Masook's security team. Then the sound of suppressed gunfire came clearly across the feed.

Shit.

Someone was shooting.

Alex looked around and tried the porthole, but it didn't

open. They were moving out of the harbor and into the Med.

Raised voices in the hallway outside made him freeze. They spoke in Arabic but he understood every word.

"You'll never work again." Masook. Who was he talking to?

"Ah, my friend, of course I will." Salamander. Shit. Alex stilled as that familiar hatred and revulsion rose up inside him. "If you're smart you'll work with me."

"With you?" Masook's tone was hostile. "For you, you mean." He was no fool.

"Working for me beats being dead, yes?" said Salamander.

"Why are you doing this? This is not how we work. Your client should have paid more," Masook complained.

"My client doesn't just want what you are offering. He wants the supplier, too."

So did Alex, but he'd find them with or without Masook.

Masook laughed sourly. "If I give you that you'll kill me for sure."

Salamander's oily reply snaked under the door. "Maybe. Maybe not."

More indistinct noises as if someone else was joining them.

"But if you don't tell me, I will kill your daughter."

Alex drew in a sharp breath.

"How sloppy to bring a child on a business trip."

Taylor shrieked. Alex closed his eyes. This op had suddenly gone to shit, and all because Charles Salamander was a treacherous backstabber. If only Alex had pulled the trigger all those years ago…

"Let me go!" Taylor Masook's yelp of pain had Alex stretching his neck from side to side. The chance of making his own wedding was getting slimmer, but Mallory wouldn't stand on this side of the door while a child was in danger.

Salamander's voice grew patronizing, and he switched to English even though Taylor spoke Arabic. "I won't hurt you, little girl. I just want something your father has."

"That's stealing! You're a bad man. Ouch, you're hurting me." She squealed again.

"Your daddy is a bad man, too. He likes to sell deadly weapons to terrorists, but you live with your delusions, child."

"You're lying. My daddy wouldn't do something like that!"

Poor kid. Her dreams were gonna get shattered one way or another, assuming she lived that long. With the laptop slung across his back Alex put his hand on the knob. Time to get rid of Salamander for good.

"I want the name of the scientist who created it else I'll put a bullet in your poor, sweet child."

Alex paused.

"Don't hurt her! I'll tell you what I know, but I don't know the name. Let me get my laptop. I will show you my correspondence and how I make payments. Just let her go. This man is easily spooked. He is terrified the FBI is watching him."

FBI? What the hell? Was this an American traitor?

"He will only deal with me. Without me you will never find him." Masook sounded desperate.

Salamander enjoyed other people's fear.

Alex's time was up. Once Masook realized the laptop was gone he'd know he'd been robbed. Who knew what Salamander would do to the kid then.

Alex came out of the room and double-tapped the goon closest to him. The nanny he'd been holding hostage slumped against the wall. Alex turned and then, before Taylor had finished drawing in breath to scream, aimed his SIG between Salamander's wide, brown eyes. He saw the flash of recognition but didn't hesitate to pull the trigger.

Click.

For the first time on a mission Alex's gun jammed. He lunged for the dead bodyguard's gun and rolled across the passageway, kicking open the nearest door as bullets followed him and peppered the thin walls behind him. Taylor screamed so high Alex thought the windows might shatter.

He cleared the SIG and checked the other gun. Both were locked and loaded.

"Ah, Mr. Parker," Salamander called. "So good to see you again after all these years. Come out and bring the samples with you and I won't kill Masook's child."

Alex pressed his lips together. All he needed was one, clear shot.

"You have three seconds. Three, two, one…"

Alex had no choice. He came out and aimed his pistol, but Salamander was completely shielded behind the nanny. Another of Salamander's henchmen held Taylor around the waist like a rag doll. Masook was nowhere to be seen.

Alex tilted his head slightly as he looked down the sights. "Hiding behind a woman, Charles?"

He caught the edge of a smile as the snake ducked back behind the terrified nanny. Maybe she *was* just the hired help.

"Ah, I missed you, Alex." Salamander seemed gleeful at this turn of events. "I had heard that you retired from your position at the CIA, but the rumors were obviously exaggerated."

The excitement in his voice crawled over Alex's flesh.

"It is a shame that I have to kill you now."

Salamander raised his pistol, but Alex shot the gun out of the man's hand. Salamander screamed in pain, but managed to wrap his injured arm around the nanny's neck, blood running down her chest and dripping onto the cream carpet. The threat was implicit. Come closer, and the nanny died.

The henchman holding Taylor raised his weapon to fire, but Alex shot him right between the eyes. The little girl screamed, and he winced. Jane would probably kill him herself for traumatizing her daughter.

A violent curse erupted from Masook's office. He was no doubt looking for the bullets to the pistol he kept in his desk drawer. Alex had them in his pocket.

Taylor scrambled away from the dead bodyguard and ran to her father.

Dammit.

Alex walked towards the man he should have killed years ago—and yet, if he had, he might never have met Mallory. Never known true joy. All that suffering had been worth it in the end.

"Let Josette go," Alex told Salamander calmly. "And I won't kill you."

Salamander laughed and glanced behind him as if expecting to be rescued. "You won't kill me. You and I are connected. In the cosmic universe, you can no more kill me than I can kill you. Why do you think I've left you alone all these years?"

"Connected?" Alex sneered. "By the scars on my back, you mean?"

"But they are just scars, my friend. You lived to tell the tale, did you not?"

If that was Salamander's idea of mercy, fuck him. Alex

took a step forward and reached the door of Masook's office. Masook held a gun pointed at him.

"Put it down if you want to live," Alex told Masook.

Shakily Masook laid the pistol on the table. Alex hadn't thought the man was that smart.

The little girl watched him with wide, terrified eyes that reminded Alex of her mother. "It's okay, Taylor. I'm not going to hurt you."

Masook's mouth dropped open. "Jane. You're working with Jane."

"Who's Jane?" Taylor asked.

Masook looked suddenly stricken.

Alex kept an eye on both Masook and Salamander. He didn't trust either of them. The nanny hadn't said a word, but she looked suitably frightened. Had he been mistaken about her?

"I'm with a joint FBI/CIA/Interpol task force. But you're right. Taylor's mother is the reason I'm here."

"My mommy is dead," Taylor said sadly.

"Did you sleep with the whore?" Masook spat.

Whoa. Lots of unresolved anger there.

Taylor's lip turned down, and she hugged herself tightly.

Alex was about to shake his head when Salamander sneered. "And you have the world believing you're madly in love with your pretty FBI agent."

Alex's world slowed and contracted down to a bullet point.

"What would you know about my pretty FBI agent?" he asked quietly.

Alex watched as Salamander eased down almost in slow motion and reached for the weapon the security guard had dropped on the floor. Alex let him do it, let him touch the cold, dull steel, let him wrap the palm of his hand around the grip.

Maybe the nanny realized Alex would shoot through her if necessary. Or she read the truth in his eyes. She dropped to her knees, and Alex squeezed the trigger in quick succession, sending two bullets through the bastard's skull. Salamander was dead before he hit the floor.

The sound of another gun going off took him by surprise. The heat of a bullet scored the flesh of his upper arm, hit the laptop on his back.

Damn. Masook must have carried some ammunition on his person.

And there was little Taylor staring up at him, and Alex was left with exactly the same conundrum that had got him into that Moroccan jail the first time—being unable to kill a man in front of his child.

Masook's finger began squeezing the trigger again, aiming at Alex's head this time. Alex leapt out of the way before the bullet slammed into the wall opposite.

Shit.

Taylor screamed again. Josette stood uncertainly in the corridor. Why the hell didn't she run?

"Get in front of me." He gestured to Josette.

"Are you going to use me as a shield, too?" she asked with an ugly twist to her lips.

"I just want you where I can see you, lady."

Masook came to the doorway, holding Taylor in front of him. Alex should shoot him just for that.

"Touch that trigger again, and I will put a bullet between your eyes, Masook," he warned the man.

Masook went white and kept his finger off the trigger

which made Alex wonder if he was out of ammo. He was definitely a lousy shot.

Alex had screwed up this op. First his gun jamming, then leaving Masook with a useable weapon.

"It doesn't matter." The nanny wet her lips. "We're all dead already."

"What?" Alex frowned.

The nanny nodded slowly to his computer bag, and Alex inched the strap around. Sure enough there was a hole where Masook's bullet had hit the plastic case and a slight dusting of white powder across the black material of the bag.

"What is it?" Alex demanded urgently.

Masook's eyes went wide, and he swayed slightly, resting his hands on his daughter's shoulders. "Quickly. Get the vaccine out. There is enough for the three of you."

"Why not you?" Alex pulled the bag over his head and placed it on the floor.

"I insisted on getting vaccinated before I'd handle the transaction."

"Anthrax?"

Masook nodded. "But a virulent and fast-acting strain. You have only minutes to live. Inject the vaccine quickly into your bloodstream and you might survive." Masook looked down at his daughter. "Stay with this man, Taylor. I will come for you one day." With that Masook turned around and ran.

Alex swore. No matter what, Masook wouldn't get far.

Taylor went to chase after her father, but Alex snagged her arm.

"Let me give you the injection first, poppet, so you don't get sick. Then we'll go find your daddy." The fucking asshole.

He opened the cracked case.

Time stilled, and a million disjointed thoughts rushed through his head before everything inside him shattered. He stared at the row of glass bottles snug in their foam inserts. The bullet had destroyed a vial of the toxin, but it had also destroyed the vial containing the liquid vaccine. His gaze met the nanny's and then he stared at the child who was looking at him with trusting, big, blue eyes even though she'd seen him kill three men in the space of a few minutes.

There wasn't any vaccine left.

He wanted to tell Taylor everything was going to be okay, but he couldn't force the lie past his lips.

If what Masook said was true, chances were Alex wouldn't get to marry Mallory this coming Saturday. Chances were he wouldn't get the opportunity to be a father, or even meet his child.

Alex was a dead man.

CHAPTER EIGHTEEN

"STEP BACK. BOTH of you." Alex carefully placed the broken case on the floor.

The most dangerous form of Anthrax infection was the inhalation type so he was careful to keep his breathing as shallow as possible although, really, if Masook was telling the truth about this being some kind of amped up version of the bacteria, chances were he was already fucked.

Minutes to live.

Well, that sucked.

He wanted to call Mallory and tell her he loved her, but there were innocents to care for and bad guys to stop. "Go into that bathroom over there and wet some towels and wrap them around your faces."

The two females disappeared into the nearby toilet and even as he stripped off his shirt and pants and laid them on top of the laptop case in the hopes of containing the spread of the spores, he allowed that sliver of despair to work its way through him. Goddamn it. He'd never imagined this mission would end this way, never imagined he'd finally have to pay for his sins. He stripped down to his boxers and checked his weapons.

He coughed as something seemed to scratch at the back of his throat and panic scrabbled at his mind. He pushed it away.

Even if he was dying he had a job to do.

He would not allow anyone to spread this disease and Masook might be immune, but he had spores all over his clothes and would spread the contamination with unknown consequences. Alex knew what he had to do. He picked up his SIG.

"Look after the child," he called out to Josette.

Alex didn't want Taylor to see her father die. She was an innocent in this nightmare and there was a good chance she was going to die soon, too. He had to hurry.

He ran up the steps, grateful he was still mobile. Who knew how violently this thing would kill him.

The lights of Antibes were already small and faded in the distance. Another good thing—less chance of the spores making landfall. As Alex approached the top deck he called Frazer.

"Everything all right?" Frazer asked.

"Not exactly." Alex forced the words past a knot in his throat.

"You have the girl?"

"She's here."

"The weapon?"

"I have it."

"Then what's the problem?"

It was getting harder to hear Frazer because of the incredibly loud noise from the helicopter's rotors.

Masook was going to make a run for it, leaving his daughter behind to possibly die a cruel and horrific death. Alex jogged faster, but the asshole was already taking off, uncaring of the fact he might spread a deadly toxin. Alex sprinted across the deck to where he'd left the guard bound and gagged earlier.

120

The man was permanently out of the game with a bullet in the back of his skull. Dammit.

Alex grabbed the gear he'd left on deck and slipped on the thin black hoodie, wincing a little at the wound where the bullet had grazed him earlier. At least it camouflaged his pale torso against the incipient blackness. He didn't bother with the protective vest. A bullet might be preferable to dying from this goddamned insidious infection.

Were the bacteria replicating in his lungs, right now? Were they multiplying through his cells?

Finally, the bird was far enough away that he could hear Frazer talking. "Listen," he cut in. "One of the toxin vials cracked open during a gunfight. According to Masook it contained a highly virulent form of anthrax." Tears pricked at Alex's eyes, and emotion made his throat ache. Or maybe he really was a soulless bastard and it was just the sharp, sea breeze.

Or maybe it was the anthrax.

"Use the damn antidote!"

He'd never heard Frazer sound panicked before. "That got shot up, too."

"Alex…" Frazer sounded grim. "I swear to God if you die, I will kill you. Get me information on the supplier. We'll get more vaccine shipped in, antibiotics… The wedding can be postponed."

God, the wedding…

After all his promises to Mallory he was going to let her down badly. Leave her to raise their child alone. He swallowed. *Get it together, jackass.* He didn't have time for weakness. He had too much to do in the little time he had left.

"Masook said we'd be dead in minutes, and that was about

five minutes ago. He's in the helicopter, covered in spores. I'm going to prevent him from spreading this stuff. Don't let anyone come onboard the *Fair Winds* unless they're in a HAZMAT suit. And do not tell Mal about this. If I don't get to talk to either of you again tell her I love her."

"Tell her yourself." Frazer sounded furious, but Alex knew him well enough to know that's how the man dealt with emotion.

Who'd have thought Alex would be the warm and fuzzy one in their relationship. "This isn't your fault, Linc."

Alex rung off and called a different number, one he'd memorized a short time ago. It only took a moment for the call to go through. The explosion turned the chopper into a fireball over the dark water, burning metal raining out of the night sky and into the Med.

That should take care of the spores.

Then he heard another sound. That of an outboard motor. Damn. He couldn't let anyone leave this boat alive. There was enough normal anthrax in one vial to kill hundreds of thousands of people. This strain was probably even more deadly.

Alex strode to the port side. Josette had lowered a small speedboat into the water.

He pointed the gun at her and fired a warning shot into the water. "I will not let you put people at risk, Josette. I will kill you."

He heard footsteps coming toward him and glanced back.

Taylor peeked over the top step. "Please don't shoot me. Josette told me to give you this. 'As an offering of good faith.'" The girl came on deck and carefully handed over a glass bottle.

Alex had a heart the size of Texas stuck in his mouth as he

took it from her. It was a vial exactly like the ones in Masook's safe.

"Did she take this out of the red case that was shot up?" he asked the kid.

Taylor shook her head. "She got it from her room. She said we weren't in any danger. She told me I wouldn't die."

Alex looked at the earnestness on Taylor's face and then stared down the length of his pistol that was still pointed at the nanny. He'd been right not to trust the woman, but it didn't make him feel any better.

He examined the vial while Josette cast off. She held up a waterproof case to show him, a case that looked exactly like the one he'd stolen from Masook's safe. Minus the bullet hole.

"I swapped out the real toxins, Mr. Parker," Josette shouted.

"What about the vaccine?" he yelled back.

"I need that for my government to replicate. But you're fine. You weren't infected. It was just cornstarch and talc!" She laughed and went to start the outboard. "I'm not the enemy, Mr. Parker. I'll get this to our labs. My government will be in touch with your government."

"Which government is that?" he demanded.

"A friendly one."

Did he believe her? Damn, he didn't know.

He wanted to. Wanted to believe he still had that future with Mallory and their child to look forward to.

His pistol wavered.

She turned up the throttle and gunned the motor, heading away fast into the night. Alex kept the SIG trained on her but, dammit, if he hit a vial, with the wind direction, he and Taylor could end up getting a face full of the spores she'd stolen. How stupid would that be? Then again, how stupid was it to watch an operative from an unknown country escape with something this potentially deadly?

Didn't matter now. She was out of range.

He lowered his weapon. Looked at the kid. "How are you feeling?"

"Good. Not sick." She bit her lip as it started to wobble. "Where is my daddy?" She was eyeing the burning wreckage of the helicopter. Orange and red flames reflected over the water.

Alex clenched his teeth. Did he lie? What was the point? "The helicopter blew up." He didn't mention it had blown up because of him. "I'm sorry."

And he was. He was truly sorry Taylor had lost her father even though Ahmed Masook had been an evil sonofabitch.

She started to cry, and he picked her up. She wrapped her arms and legs around him, clinging like a baby monkey. He stuffed his pistol into the hoodie pocket, keeping a firm grip on the vial even as his heart pounded. He needed to find a safe place to store this sucker.

He gave Taylor a squeeze and let her go. "Come on, kid. We have work to do."

She followed him up to the bridge. He needed to figure out if there was anyone else alive on the boat and wanted a clear view of the surrounding area in case anyone else came to visit.

The bridge was empty, the boat set to autopilot.

Salamander had organized a coup, killing off Masook's security probably by bribing a couple of guards on Masook's team. Salamander had probably intended to escape via the helicopter or another boat. Alex doubted any of the rest of the crew had survived. He made a mental note to check on the other security guard he'd left unconscious when he'd first come aboard.

The carnage made it clear there was no way Salamander would have let Masook live. Alex didn't like to think about what would have happened to Taylor after Salamander had gotten what he wanted out of Masook.

Alex found a small fridge on the bridge and carefully placed the vial inside. Finally, he called Frazer.

"The nanny escaped on a speedboat," Alex told him. Someone, Matt presumably, should have spotted the woman already. A small flotilla of boats was approaching the helicopter wreckage that now lay behind them. "Josette claims she has the real toxin and left a sample with me as an act of faith." Alex cleared his throat. "She said she'd swapped out the original vials and that we hadn't been infected."

"Do you believe her?"

"I want to." Desperately. "She had an identical case to the one Masook had in his safe and the vials look the same. She said her government would be in touch."

"So that's what she was there for? All very James Bond," Frazer commented dryly. Alex heard relief edge Frazer's tone, but they weren't in the clear yet.

"We can't risk she's lying." Alex said softy. "You need to arrange someone to follow 'Josette' or pick her up. You need to arrange a cordon around this boat." He frowned at all the controls. "I need to figure out how to drop the anchor."

"I know how." Taylor showed him a lever on the bridge.

"You want to do the honors?" Alex asked her.

Taylor nodded.

"The girl is safe?" asked Frazer.

She appeared fine as far as Alex could tell. Minus the emotional trauma. "As safe as I am."

TONI ANDERSON

"What do you want me to do?" asked Frazer.

"Keep the cops and press and everyone else away from us. Arrange an airdrop of airtight body bags. Get a group from the French equivalent of the CDC out here so they can confirm we don't have anthrax in our systems. I suspect the boat has everything we'll need to survive a few days until we get confirmation."

"Roger that."

"And start finding out who in the US is working on anthrax as a bioweapon."

"US?" Frazer sounded terse.

"That's what I inferred from what Masook said."

"I assume he was the firework I saw a few minutes ago."

"Affirmative." Alex watched the tearstained face of the child and wished she hadn't had to endure what she had over the last hour. Josette had played him. Assuming they weren't exposed to a bioweapon. She'd known Alex would try to stop Masook and that had given her time to make her escape. If he had to guess who she worked for, he'd say the Mossad, but he didn't like guessing.

"Salamander?" Frazer asked.

"Pretty sure everyone else onboard the *Fair Winds* is dead. Salamander must have had people inside Masook's security team. They killed the others and probably all the crew. It was only a matter of time before they killed Masook and..." He stopped talking and cleared his throat. Taylor was in hearing distance.

"Jane is going to want to come onboard," Frazer said softly.

Alex thought about it. If he was in her position and the person he loved most in the world was on this boat, he'd want to be here, too. Even if it killed him.

"Maybe you should let her." It was up to her whether or not she wanted to risk her life. "And do not tell Mallory about this. Complete radio silence."

"What if you get sick—"

"Especially if I get sick. She'll fly out and swim to the boat if she has to. No way. Even if she wasn't pregnant, no fucking way. No one tells her anything to stress her out. As far as she is concerned I'm undercover and will be back in plenty of time for the wedding."

"What if she asks me directly?"

"Then you lie. Promise me, Linc."

"I promise. But the press might get hold of this."

"Don't let them."

Frazer laughed. "You seem to have a high opinion of my abilities, friend. You better get those bodies off the deck and in the freezer, pronto."

Frazer obviously had a view of the deck, and Alex spotted the *Ascension* just to the north of them.

"Good point." Alex just smiled. "I need to check for survivors…"

"Okay. Try not to scare the kid to death."

"I'll try."

"Alex…"

"If you declare undying love for me I might have to shoot you."

Frazer laughed. "Just wanted to say thanks for trusting me with best man duties. I take my vows very seriously. I will get you to the church on time."

"Assuming I don't die."

"Assuming you don't die," Frazer confirmed.

"Just…" Alex drew a long breath in then released it. "If anything does happen to me…take care of Mallory for me."

"That's a given."

"And *that's* why you're my best man. I'm going to need you to do something else for me…"

"What is it?"

"What's your handwriting like?"

CHAPTER NINETEEN

I T WAS DAWN and a slight wind ruffled her hair and raised goosebumps on her arms. Jane sat in the middle of a small inflatable dingy staring at Reilly who was escorting her out to the *Fair Winds*.

He wore shorts and a soft, gray t-shirt. Frazer wanted appearances to reflect people on vacation in the south of France, not personnel protection embroiled in national security matters. The t-shirt had some sort of beer logo on the front and clung very nicely to a wall of muscle in the face of the prevailing wind.

"What?" he asked when he caught her staring at him.

"Nothing."

The Saudi billionaire wanted his yacht back, but there was the matter of bioweapons and dead arms dealers and security guards to deal with first. French naval vessels formed a distant perimeter ostensibly investigating the helicopter crash, but also keeping other boats away from the two super-yachts.

The French had rounded up all the wannabe terrorists off the streets last night, including three Russians who'd tried to flee via the local airport when something had gone wrong with their boat's engine. No one was admitting anything, but one of the Brits, Noah Zacharias, had a grin on his face every time the Russians were mentioned.

The French were taking the lead on the anthrax investigation. Lincoln Frazer hadn't liked it, but he hadn't complained too much. Probably because Alex was currently delving into Masook's computer with or without the French government's permission.

It had been six hours since Alex and Taylor had possibly been infected with anthrax, but they hadn't become sick yet. It didn't mean they weren't sick, just that they weren't sick *yet*. Jane was holding on to hope. It looked more and more likely that the bioweapon either wasn't as virulent as advertised, or had been swapped out for something innocuous by the nanny who'd gotten away. Her boat had been found a few miles down the coast, but no vials. And, despite having good images of the woman and voice data, there was no record of her in any system.

"You should wait another few hours. Just to make sure there isn't any anthrax on that boat," Reilly spoke just loudly enough to be heard over the small outboard motor. He hadn't wanted her to come, but he was bringing her anyway.

"I can't." Jane looked up at the clear sky and the incredible beauty of the region. If today was her last, at least she'd die with great scenery. And if today was Taylor's last day, she wanted to hold her child in her arms, one more time, even if it meant certain death.

The tang of salt was strong on the air. Gulls circled above them.

Reilly maneuvered them expertly alongside the hull of the *Fair Winds*, grabbing one end of the ladder that extended up the side of the yacht. He tied off the boat and offered her his hand.

She scrubbed her damp palm over her thigh before standing awkwardly, trying not to tip them.

This might be the last time she saw him, she realized suddenly. She took his hand, warm, strong fingers curling around hers, a shock of awareness blasting through her. Not just attraction—something else. Something deeper. She blinked back tears. "I didn't believe men like you existed," she confessed.

He raised a brow over those calm eyes. He opened his mouth but she cut him off.

"Thank you. I wouldn't have gotten through this nightmare without you looking out for me." She wished she could have asked for more. Maybe a hug, or a farewell kiss. Despite what he'd said to her about teaching her to defend herself, she doubted she'd see him again when this was all over. He'd move on to another job, another client, and she'd—hopefully—have her hands full relearning how to be a mother.

His lips firmed, and he nodded. "Hold on tight to the ladder as the boat moves around a bit in the swell."

She curled her fingers over the metal rungs and felt his hands brush the curve of her waist as he helped her start her journey. Once onboard there was no going back until the boat was cleared by the French officials.

She hesitated. "Take care, Jack."

"You, too." His fingers tightened. Alex had ordered him not to leave the inflatable and to get back to the *Ascension* as fast as possible. She didn't want him exposed to danger. He'd done more than enough, bringing her over here.

Her throat got tight with all the things she wanted to say that were not professional and far from appropriate. She gritted her teeth and started climbing, refusing to look back. It was on that long climb up the ladder she finally allowed herself to think about meeting her daughter again. The idea Taylor might die because of her actions wasn't lost on her—except— she hadn't been the one selling germ warfare. And the Moroccan had been the one to betray Masook, not her.

Taylor would still have suffered even if Jane hadn't asked Alex for help. In fact, she'd probably already be dead.

If Taylor died…

Jane shoved the thought out of her mind. She wouldn't die. Jane wouldn't allow it. She climbed what seemed to be the world's tallest ladder and refused to think about the height. Heights and ladders were not her thing but nothing would keep her from her baby. Except, maybe fear and loathing from Taylor herself…

Finally, Jane got to the top and a hand came over the rail to help her. Alex Parker. Who'd risked everything for a woman he didn't even like when he was on the cusp of a wedding to his pregnant sweetheart.

He lifted her aboard and gave a wave to Jack, still waiting at the bottom of the ladder.

She waved too, wishing for things she couldn't have from a man she shouldn't want.

Then she braced herself and looked around the deck. No sign of Taylor.

"I didn't tell her you were coming. In case you changed your mind." Alex had stripped off his shirt and was wearing what looked like cutoff pants.

"How are you feeling?" she asked him.

His skin looked tanned and healthy except for a bandage wrapped around his one arm. There was sweat on his chest, but not the pallor of sickness. Just the gleam of hard, physical labor. She knew he'd been moving bodies so anyone doing a flyby wouldn't see anything was amiss.

He grinned, white teeth flashing and matching the eerie paleness of his silver eyes. "I feel good. And Taylor seems fine, too. It doesn't mean we're out of the woods…"

But it was a good sign.

A hand came up onto the railing behind her and Jane startled. A moment later, Reilly was on deck beside them, taking everything in with a few sweeping looks.

"I thought I told you to head back to the other yacht?" Alex said.

Reilly put his hands on his hips. "Thought I'd take a few vacation days."

Alex huffed out a laugh. "On a vessel that is potentially contaminated with anthrax?"

Reilly gave his boss a smile, and Jane's heart sped up. "I've had my jabs. Anyway, I didn't do it for you, boss. I did it for Jane. But now that I'm here you may as well put me to work. Jane and her daughter have a lot of catching up to do."

Jane swallowed the tightness in her throat and reached to take Reilly's hand. He squeezed her fingers. "Thank you."

Alex blew out a big breath but didn't look happy.

"French version of the CDC will be here in the next hour. They'll start top to bottom decontamination as well as take blood samples from each of us and give us massive doses of just-in-case antibiotics. They'll have people autopsying the bodies in one of the big walk-in refrigerators in the galley. And they'll be analyzing the powder directly."

"I'm sorry for getting you mixed up in this, Alex," she told him.

He looked at her. "We helped get a great many evil people off the streets last night."

She swallowed. "But still…"

Alex shook his head. "Whatever guilt you're harboring, forget it. Charles Salamander knew about Mallory." His eyes held that light she recognized from when they'd worked together for The Gateway Project. "As soon as I discovered that, he had to die." A cold smile curved his lips. "At least this way I got to kill him in a fair fight without fear of spending the next twenty years in prison. It's done. Mallory's safe, and that's all I really care about. Go find your daughter. She's watching TV in the main salon. No dead bodies in there."

Jane nodded uncertainly, and Reilly rested a hand on Alex's shoulder as she walked away.

It wasn't hard to find the salon. Taylor was lying on the carpet in front of the TV. She'd fallen asleep watching a *Beauty and the Beast* DVD. The terror of the night before had caught up with her.

Jane ached. She stared at the sun-streaked, blonde hair held back with a black band. Long, thin limbs sprawled, arms cradling her head.

Was she breathing? Jane took a step forward, but suddenly Taylor's back rose in a slow, steady motion. Jane paused in relief and swallowed. She kicked off her shoes and quietly padded across the floor. Despite being desperate to talk to her daughter, she didn't want to wake her from a restful sleep. Jane sank to her knees and placed a gentle hand on the child's back. Taylor didn't waken, but she did snuggle up closer to Jane's legs.

Jane sent up a prayer, thanking God for allowing her this moment. Even if Taylor died, or she died, Jane felt like she'd finally come home. She glanced up and there was Reilly, staring at her through the open doorway. He smiled and she saw something in his eyes that made her blink. Admiration. And maybe something else. Something…honest. Something pure.

Tentatively she smiled back. She didn't know what would happen when they got off this boat, but he'd come with her on this journey at great risk to himself. Maybe he'd done it for Alex too, because she knew he had a great deal of regard for his boss. But Reilly wasn't an impetuous man. He was strong, reliable, and understood that her priority right now was her child. He'd come anyway.

He grinned at her, and hot tears gathered in her eyes, which she blinked quickly away. No crying was allowed. Suddenly, Taylor rolled over and opened her eyes.

"Who are you?" she asked softly, eyes wide with wonder.

Jane held her breath and opened her mouth. She had practiced introducing herself a thousand times, but all that preparation fell away in the moment. "I'm your mommy."

Taylor's young face pinched in confusion. She'd lost all her baby roundness and had grown tall and lean. Tears had left white lines on her cheeks—she must have cried herself to sleep earlier. "Daddy said you were dead."

Jane reached out very slowly and moved a piece of Taylor's hair off her cheek. "Daddy got very mad with me and wouldn't let me see you anymore." She asked the question that had burned a hole in her soul. "Do you remember me?"

Taylor grabbed her hand and held on tight. "Yes, I just don't know if you're real or if I'm dreaming."

Relief hit her. "I'm real." Those fingers wrapped around Jane's heart and squeezed. "Your daddy made a mistake, Taylor." Jane would save the blame for another day when their child's grief wasn't so fresh. "He wanted you to be with him, not me."

Taylor sat up. "Where were you?"

Jane was desperate to touch, to grab hold and never let go, but she didn't want to frighten or overwhelm Taylor. "I was looking for you. Every single day, I was looking for you."

Taylor wiped the back of her hand across her cheeks while Jane held her breath. Taylor launched herself against her, and Jane wrapped her arms around her baby. Jane held on so damn tight it was a wonder she didn't suffocate the child.

Taylor's sobs filled the air, great bursting bouts of pure grief. Jane rocked her, rejoicing at her warmth, at the rapid heartbeat thudding against her ribs. She looked up. Reilly watched them with bright eyes. Alex stood behind him with a small smile on his lips.

She smiled back. Funny. She wasn't scared of him anymore.

"Thank you," she mouthed.

He nodded and turned away.

She caught Reilly's gaze. She didn't say anything but let her gratitude for him shine through, along with an acknowledgement of the attraction that simmered between them. She didn't know if it would come to anything, but it was honest and pure. Not based on wealth, or the need to punish herself. It deserved a chance.

Starting something up right now was probably the dumbest thing either of them could do, but she didn't care. She wanted to crawl into bed with Jack Reilly and sleep in his embrace. It didn't need to be more complicated or difficult than that. And if they survived this thing that was exactly what she intended to do.

CHAPTER TWENTY

THE HANDHELD PROPULSION device that dragged Alex beneath the surface of the water might have been a lot more fun if he hadn't had to share it with an ugly-ass Navy SEAL. The water was cold, and his teeth clamped hard onto his regulator so they didn't start chattering. He caught sight of Jane holding on tight to another Navy SEAL and little Taylor was flying along with yet another. Jack was there, too.

When French police stepped onboard in a few days' time they'd find it empty except for the dead bodies in the refrigerator. Tests had been done, everything had come back clean. They hadn't been exposed to anything deadlier than cornstarch.

But the French had stood by the seven-day quarantine rule they'd imposed, and Alex refused to wait that long. He was getting married in just over thirteen hours, and the entire Atlantic stood between him and his intended. He wasn't going to sit around here while French authorities added this arbitrary time span just because they could. If it had a scientific basis, if he'd thought there was even the slightest risk, Alex would have stayed put. But it didn't, and he wasn't going to get caught up in red tape or endless legal enquiries when he had promises to keep.

The bottom scraped his knees, and the SEAL turned the

submersible off as they reached shallow water. Alex popped his head above the surface and dragged off his mask. "Thanks, man." He shook the SEAL's hand.

"Anytime." The frogman grinned. "That was fun."

On shore, a small group of people stood staring at them. Alex spotted Frazer motioning him to move it. Alex staggered out of the surf, trying to avoid the sharp rocks with his bare feet. Frazer grabbed his arm and dragged him to a nearby car and virtually threw him into the backseat.

"Drive," Frazer ordered.

"Nice to see you, too." Alex tried to catch his breath.

The driver floored the engine and they shot away, fishtailing and spitting grit. Alex glanced behind them. Reilly, Jane and Taylor were being bundled into a second vehicle. Obviously, Frazer wanted to brief him alone.

Water ran off his t-shirt and board shorts, soaking the upholstery. They sped past the rocky outcrops as the driver really booted it.

"Think we can make it?"

"We better," Frazer said dryly. "Greenburg lent us his new Gulfstream G-650. It does over seven-hundred miles an hour and will get us to Virginia in nine and a half hours. That gives us an hour's drive time when we get there."

Alex looked down at his attire. "I don't have my tux."

"It's all been taken care of. Some of the others went ahead yesterday and took those damned place cards with them. Why didn't you have them printed for god's sake?"

"Apparently, it's more *authentic* to write your own."

Frazer rolled his eyes. "Remind me not to hire your wedding planner."

Alex grinned. Frazer ignored him and carried on, "We'll

have three cars with drivers and a police escort waiting for us at Reagan National. Clothes for the wedding party should be in each of the cars. Ashley's, yours and mine. We can change in the cars on the way."

Frazer took a phone call and Alex stared out the window. He had a feeling it would be a long time before he visited the region again. "Does Mallory know what happened?"

"No."

"I should have told her."

"No." Frazer said sharply. "You shouldn't. You only got the one hundred percent all-clear two hours ago and we hadn't got you off the boat yet. There was no guarantee we'd get here at all. Now we just have to navigate a few thousand miles."

"I promised her I wouldn't ever lie to her again."

"You didn't have a choice."

Alex was emotionally exhausted. "Are the French going to try to stop us?"

Frazer grinned. "We helped them catch a bunch of terrorists and prevented a bioweapon being sold on French soil. We made them look like heroes. We can just as easily make them look like incompetent assholes, and they know it."

"Did you track Josette?"

"Officially? No. Unofficially the Mossad reached out to some IC connections and suggested the samples were in friendly hands."

The Mossad was better than a terrorist group, but Alex still didn't like it. "Figure out who the seller is yet?"

Frazer shook his head. "Nope. But the list of potential suspects is small. We'll catch them."

They screeched into a small private airstrip, and the car drove right up to the steps of the sleek-looking jet and jerked to a halt. The other car pulled up behind them.

Frazer virtually dragged Alex out of the car and up the steps of the airplane. Jane and the others jogged quickly after them.

Once they were onboard, the door was immediately closed and the steps rolled away. Alex nodded to Ashley who smiled back at him. No sign of the others. Presumably they'd returned to the States. The jet immediately started taxiing. Someone had thoughtfully placed several thick towels over the seats so they wouldn't ruin the soft leather.

"Someone is taking their best man duties very seriously," Alex noted wryly as Frazer sank down beside him.

One side of the man's lips curled. "What can I say? I *am* the best man."

Alex glanced across the aisle at Reilly and Jane who were holding hands. Taylor sat grinning and looking around in excitement. She'd bounced back remarkably quickly despite everything that had happened. Being reunited with a mother whom she'd thought she'd lost had definitely eased the pain of her father's death. And Masook had been a hard man, not given to overt displays of affection.

Alex wasn't sorry he was dead. He was only sorry Taylor had seen the helicopter wreckage and understood what it had meant.

"Would you like to come to my wedding?" he asked her as the plane reared up into the sky.

Taylor's eyes went wide, and she nodded. He'd spent the last few days telling the girl all about Mallory and the baby and their dog, Rex. Jane and Reilly obviously meant something to one another, and Reilly was coming to the wedding. Why not Jane and Taylor, too?

Jane looked down at her clothes with a grimace. "We have

nothing to wear."

He thought about the conversation he'd had with Mallory about clothes. It seemed like a million years ago now. "I don't care what you wear. You can come like that."

Jane gaped at him.

"I fetched all your belongings from the chateau so you have dry clothes you can change into just as soon as we reach cruising height," Frazer said patiently. "You can give me your sizes and my beautiful and amazing partner will arrange something for the ceremony. She has excellent taste." Frazer flashed Jane a smile.

"Think I should call Mallory?" Alex asked quietly.

"It's three a.m. her time the night before her wedding. Let her sleep. Send her a text and say you're on your way."

"A text?"

"It's an electronic message they use on phones."

"Funny."

"I thought so."

"Good thing I don't have my gun." Alex had thrown it over the side of the *Fair Winds* to avoid any possible murder charges.

"Temper temper."

"Lincoln?"

"What?" Frazer turned and looked him in the eye.

"I love you, man."

Frazer shook his head in disgust. "Get yourself tidied up before you embarrass yourself."

They reached cruising altitude, and Alex immediately undid his seatbelt and stood, grabbing Frazer's head and kissing him on the top of it. He ruffled the man's perfectly trimmed hair. "I know you love me, too. You're repressed. You'll figure it out eventually."

CHAPTER TWENTY-ONE

I T WAS SEVEN a.m., and Mallory's girlfriends had been doing a good job of keeping her company, but now they were both sleeping after staying up late talking. Ashley wasn't here yet.

Mallory couldn't sleep.

The newborn sun glowed pink and yellow as it peeked over the nearby wooded hills, making long shadows stretch over the endless rows of short vines. The vineyard buildings and the small elegant hotel were behind her. In front of her a couple of houses were dotted around the rural valley, but no one else appeared to be awake. The houses looked like little oases of tranquility.

She was wearing rubber boots caked in mud, and was dressed in maternity jeans and a pretty pink cotton tunic and a gray cable sweater to fight the early morning chill.

Rex ran on, sniffing every other vine. Cobwebs sparkled with diamonds of fresh dew and birds sang a morning chorus that should have cheered her heart. The dog darted off after a rabbit and she followed him down the valley, into the thin mist that clung to her cheeks in a cool film.

Something was very wrong.

Mallory had texted Alex regularly this week and he had assured her he would be home in time for the wedding, but there had been something elusive in his messages that troubled her. And he still wasn't here.

It just wasn't like him.

Leaving her alone like this wasn't like him.

Equally concerning was that Frazer and Ashley were out of town. Were they all together? Were they aiding Alex in his search for Jane Sanders's daughter? Or were they busy doing other things?

They all had important jobs. She understood that. The world didn't stop just because she'd decided to get married, but...

Jed Brennan had given her various vague explanations about where her co-workers were and what they were up to. He'd sounded more and more strained in his answers. She couldn't shake the unease that Jed was lying to her. They were all lying to her.

Her teeth clenched.

Jed had also piled on the work this week, and she'd barely had time to breathe let alone worry. She'd worried anyway. She was good at multitasking.

The rehearsal dinner had been canceled. Half the wedding party were absent and there hadn't seemed much point. Didn't matter. They could wing the ceremony just as long as everyone turned up.

She caught a drop of dew on her finger from a small green leaf. She didn't doubt Alex's love or devotion, but there was something he wasn't telling her. She just didn't know what it was. Or maybe she was being naïve.

She pulled the leaf off a vine and rubbed it between her fingers, inhaling the fresh, fragrant scent.

Maybe Alex had arrived in France and realized how clingy

Mallory was. Or the idea of settling down with a wife and child was too much pressure for a former assassin. Or maybe he'd been pulled back into his old life and liked the excitement of it. Or he didn't know how to extricate himself from a certain situation or was burdened with that old insecurity that he wasn't good enough for her, which was bullshit.

No more lies...

They'd made a promise to one another while waiting for her sister's body to be uncovered in the woods behind Mallory's childhood home. No more lies. It was the only vow that truly mattered to her. What if Alex had broken that vow before they'd even got started on their lives together?

Could she trust him?

The question bothered her as much as the answer.

The wedding ceremony was set to take place in the gardens at the back of the hotel. The forecast was for a perfect, spring day full of sunshine and good cheer. Chairs were being set out in neat little rows and an arbor was being filled and covered with living plants and fresh flowers even as she walked across the bare earth between the twisted vines. The reception would be held in the massive tasting room, closed to the public for the weekend.

They'd gone for a lilac and gray color scheme with a "rustic elegance" theme, whatever that meant. To her it meant less worrying about the details. To the wedding planner it apparently meant something else entirely.

She strode through the vineyards just bursting into life, determined to walk herself out of her funk. After another mile, she turned around and headed back toward the vineyard. The soil felt good under her boots. The baby kicked in agreement and she smiled. He or she was the reason she'd changed her mind about getting married sooner rather than later. She and Alex might not be the most traditional couple, but she wanted them to be traditional in this.

The baby turned inside her, and Mallory figured he or she sensed her unease. She placed her hand on her bump.

He'd be here. Alex loved her as much as she loved him. She trusted him, she realized, without reservation. Wedding jitters had gotten the better of her, and she was worried about him.

A twig snapped, and she looked up sharply. She hid her disappointment as her mother stepped into view through the vines.

"Couldn't sleep?" Margret Tremont asked worriedly.

Mallory paused and stretched out her aching back, not answering the question. "Figured I'd get some exercise before all the madness starts."

Her mother wore a blue sweater and black leggings and tall, black boots. Her skin glowed with health and vitality though her eyes held questions. Questions Mallory didn't want to answer.

She began walking, hoping movement could somehow delay the inevitable. No such luck.

"Where's Alex? The groom is usually here by now." Her mother's voice was quiet, yet carried across the valley on the thin, morning air.

"He'll be here." Mallory spoke with more confidence than she felt.

"What if he isn't?" the senator pressed.

"Then he'll be late for his own wedding."

"Why haven't we seen him all week?" Margret Tremont was nothing if not determined.

Mallory didn't answer.

"You're willing to risk public humiliation if he doesn't turn up?"

"Yes, Mom. I'll risk the nebulous concept of humiliation by not assuming the worst and by getting ready for my own wedding because he will be here." And he would. He loved her, she knew he did. She swallowed the knot of emotion that wanted to form. Her true fear wasn't that he was going to jilt her at their wedding. What if something had happened to him? Something terrible, and she was here worrying about a stupid ceremony?

Were the others trying to help him? Trying to find him? Why wouldn't anyone tell her anything?

Mallory suddenly wanted to cry. She wanted to curl up in a ball and sob. But she would not break down. Not until she knew for certain. She had more faith than that.

Pregnancy hormones were a bitch.

She tipped up her chin and whistled for her dog. Then she took her mother's hand.

"Alex will be here." Mallory touched her heart with their joined hands, hoping that sheer force of will would make it happen. "Let's go get breakfast and start getting ready for our big day."

CHAPTER TWENTY-TWO

"**F**UCK. WE ARE never going to make it."

"*Au contraire, mon ami.*" Frazer told him, doing up the buttons of his dove-gray waistcoat and then shrugging into his hand-tailored jacket. "We are almost there."

Alex had showered and shaved on the flight back. He'd even managed a few hours' sleep. Getting ready for his wedding in the back of a black sedan while being driven at a high speed with a police escort was not something he had ever imagined when envisioning his wedding.

"You have the rings?" he asked Frazer.

Frazer frowned and searched his jacket pockets one after another and looked up with horror. Then he grinned and pulled out a jeweler's box. He snapped it open to reveal two gleaming platinum bands.

"You picked now to develop a sense of humor?" Alex asked him, trying to control his heartbeat.

Frazer's lips quirked. "Wait until you hear my best man's speech."

Alex groaned.

Frazer leaned over into the front passenger seat, pulled out another box, this one a small cooler box. He opened it and inside were two roses of the palest lilac color.

"Boutonnieres," Alex said stupidly. He'd forgotten about

the boutonnieres.

"Izzy made sure we had everything we needed."

"Izzy is a gem."

"Goddess," Frazer corrected.

Alex raised his brows. High praise indeed coming from the consummate professional who'd unexpectedly become his closest friend.

"Izzy is a goddess." The woman had saved Alex's ass, and he wasn't about to argue.

They were zooming down quiet back roads and Alex realized they were close to the vineyard. They were gonna make it.

"Get them to turn the sirens off. It's going to freak Mallory out otherwise."

Frazer nodded and called someone. The sirens turned off, and the cars slowed down to a less dangerous speed. Alex checked his watch as Frazer attached first his own buttonhole, and then Alex's.

"Any regrets? Second thoughts?" Frazer asked, smoothing Alex's lapel. They'd gone with classic black tuxes that could be worn for other occasions. Mallory was practical if nothing else.

One side of Alex's mouth twisted. "Only that I didn't get here faster."

Frazer gave a satisfied smile and leaned back. "We prevented a major biological weapons deal and got Jane Sanders her daughter back. And we made it home in time for the wedding. I think we did a damn good job."

And then the sign for the vineyard came into view, and Alex felt his pulse settle for the first time in days. A deep sense of calm washed over him. He was here. He'd made it.

CHAPTER TWENTY-THREE

MALLORY COULD SEE the anxious glances her mother and father exchanged. Two of her bridesmaids were equally nervous and the third conspicuous by her absence. Haley was waiting with the other groomsmen, last seen flirting with one of Alex's old Army pals.

Mallory stood in a side annex of the hotel. They'd completely commandeered the whole place for the wedding. The wedding planner stood near the arched wooden doors keeping anyone from wandering in.

It was five minutes to two o'clock.

The setting was fantastic, everything she'd hoped for in a venue. Beautiful but not ostentatious. Warm but elegant. Friendly. It was only missing one vital ingredient.

The groom.

"You look beautiful," her father said quietly.

Mal smoothed one hand over her baby bump and squeezed his arm with her other. "Thank you." Her gown was a wonderfully romantic affair with an embroidered lace bodice, a high waist to accommodate the baby, and layers of soft tulle with a court train. Not puffy or fussy. She'd fallen in love with it the moment she tried it on. She hoped Alex liked it. She tried to swallow, but her mouth was too dry.

She wore a circlet of flowers in her hair and had opted not

to wear a veil.

No more secrets.

"Mallory…" her mother began with another anxious glance at her father.

"Go take your seat, Mom," Mallory insisted firmly to the senator with a pointed stare at her former boss, Art Hanrahan. He gave her a nod and took her mother's arm, leading her away and out the rear entrance to where the two hundred guests were gathered.

It was a lot of people. Her mother was worried she'd be humiliated, but if Alex didn't turn up, her guests would be the least of her concerns. If Alex didn't turn up something awful must have happened. She couldn't bear the idea.

She thought she heard sirens in the distance, but then they stopped, and she decided she'd been imagining it. She walked over to where the bouquets were carefully arranged on the table. The photographer had taken a million photographs of them earlier along with photos of her with her parents and the bridesmaids. She had a horrible feeling the expression on her face would have been pensive rather than joyous but hopefully they could do some retakes later. When Alex arrived.

She reached out and touched a soft petal. A mix of pink, blush, lilac and white roses, peonies, and anemones filled out her bouquet and the scent was incredible. She wanted to find a way to remember that smell forever.

Three minutes to two o'clock.

They'd stuck to all the major traditions.

Something old—she'd had the two platinum signet rings she and her sister had once worn melted down to form a new ring which she wore on the pinky finger of her left hand.

Something new—her dress, shoes and underwear were all

new. She had a new pair of converse trainers for later if her shoes became uncomfortable. The dress was so long no one would notice, and if they did, she didn't really care. She could pretend to be hip for a day.

Something borrowed—the diamond studs in her ears were her mother's pride and joy and could probably be sold to feed a third world country for a day. Mallory was glad for the security.

Something blue—she'd had the word "blue" embroidered in blue silk on her panties. She wasn't leaving anything to chance.

One minute to two o'clock.

She walked over to the sideboard and picked up her bouquet. Her bridesmaids looked at one another.

"But Alex isn't here yet," Anna, one of her bridesmaids, cautioned.

Mallory nodded. "He'll be here."

He'd promised her he would be. He wouldn't jilt her at the altar. She had to trust him.

"Daddy," she said quietly, inclining her head to one of the men she loved most in the world. She smiled at her bridesmaids, looked over to the wedding planner. "Let's get this thing started."

Her father drew in a deep breath and seemed to realize she meant to go through with the ceremony despite the fact the groom was missing. The wedding planner looked stricken but squared her shoulders and disappeared for a moment. Strains of "Mendelssohn's Wedding March" started playing.

Mallory straightened her spine and took her father's arm. They walked quietly to the entrance just as Ashley Chen came flying through the front door of the hotel. Her gown—lilac tulle with a tight, ruched fitted bodice and spaghetti straps—was hitched up to her waist so she could run more easily. Mallory didn't know how she did it in the silver heels she wore, but she managed. Ashley dropped her skirts and the wedding planner smoothed them out and fluffed her black hair which was loose around her shoulders. There was a slight blush to her cheeks and a sparkle in her eye. The woman looked beautiful, but more important, she was here.

A wave of relief rushed over Mallory when she saw her fellow FBI agent arrive. She knew that meant Alex was here, too. Just like he'd promised.

The wedding planner appeared with Ashley's bouquet and hustled her friends towards the rear door of the hotel and out into the garden.

Her father patted her hand. "Are you all right, love?"

Mallory looked up at him. "I am now."

And they stepped out to face the congregation.

CHAPTER TWENTY-FOUR

A LEX, FRAZER, AND Lucas made it to their places at the front of the crowd with one minute to spare. That was cutting things a little fine.

Was Mallory still here or had she left in disgust? He wouldn't blame her one bit. For all she knew he'd ditched her, or had been lying to her all along. Or was just an asshole, and she'd wised up and changed her mind.

Frazer turned him around by the shoulder and gave him a thorough onceover. "Not bad, considering."

Alex laughed and shook hands quickly with all his guys and Haley who was looking unimpressed with his tardiness.

Her hair was arranged in fancy curls and she wore a long, dove-gray dress held up with thin straps.

He kissed her cheek. "You look lovely."

She let out a long-suffering sigh. "You must be hellish good in bed for Mallory to put up with your nonsense."

"Was there ever any doubt?"

"I guess not." She touched his cheek and blinked rapidly before turning away. Haley wasn't one for mushy talk.

Cherry blossoms on the nearby trees trembled on the slight breeze. He glanced around the crowd. Matt and Scarlett were back. Tanned. Happy. Grinning like lazy loons. Scarlett's parents were here, too, at Alex's invitation. Richard Stone was still battling cancer and had lost most of his hair, but the treatment seemed to be working for now. Killion and the cute and feisty Audrey Lockhart sat holding hands. Izzy Campbell and her sister Kit sat beside the spook. Darsh Singh and Erin Donovan completed that row. Some of his favorite people.

Alex nodded to Darsh, a man who'd saved his sanity and probably a lot more on the first day of the year. Sam Walker, Bradley Tate, Moira Henderson were in attendance, as were Dermot's and Haley's families.

Steve McKenzie, whom Alex had helped foil a domestic terrorism plot back in March, had his arm around Tess Fallon who'd been badly injured during the same event. Tess sent him a tentative smile which he returned. There was no sign of a wheelchair or crutches, which was a good indication she had recovered from her ordeal. She probably felt as comfortable as he did surrounded by all these politicians and law enforcement officers.

Jed Brennan grinned at him from where he sat with Vivi and Michael. Lucas's family took up two rows—the Rooneys and the Randalls were old family friends—and Becca, the girl Lucas and Ashley had saved in Boston earlier that year, sat next to Lucas's nieces, all of them giggling madly.

That was good to see.

Mallory's mom sat in the front row. As he eyed her worried expression, Alex felt a pang for what he'd put her through. He walked over and gave her a kiss on the forehead. "Sorry, Margret."

She closed her eyes and when she opened them again they were full of unshed tears. "I'm going to buy you a new watch for Christmas, Alex."

He grinned and went to stand next to Frazer again. He'd

made it. He could barely believe he'd made it. Jane Sanders caught his eye, and she sent him a grateful smile as she slipped into a chair at the back of the congregation. Reilly gripped her hand, and she held onto Taylor's. Alex wasn't sure she'd ever let the kid go again, but that was their problem. At least Ahmed Masook was permanently out of the picture.

The string quartet started playing the wedding march, and Alex felt a nervous flutter inside his chest cavity like bird's wings unfolding against his ribs. He was never nervous, but today he was. Nervous that Mallory might hate and despise him. Nervous that she might change her mind.

There was a flash of movement near the hotel doors.

"Face front, Parker," Frazer ordered.

For once, Alex did as he was told.

He stared at the minister who was giving him a look that spoke of a possible case of indigestion.

The bridesmaids came first, peeling off to stand on his left.

He heard people gasping and wondered if Mallory had taken him at his word and shown up naked, painted green. He wouldn't care. He squared his shoulders as he sensed her coming up the aisle and turned to face her.

Their gazes met, and the wind was knocked out of his chest. Instead of angry and accusing, those whiskey eyes of hers were soft and full of love.

She looked so beautiful. Tall, slender—from the front anyway—dark hair gleaming with pretty flowers. Her dress made his mouth go dry. She looked like a princess, like a nymph or a goddess.

She arrived at his side, and the scent of her and the bouquet hit him in a wave of something fresh and exquisite. He loved everything about her. She was all he'd ever wanted and rather than being here for her, he'd let her down.

Her father placed her hand over his. Her fingers were warm, her grip firm. He couldn't stop looking at her.

Slowly she smiled and then turned away to face the minister, and he followed her lead.

He spoke the words that would bind them in the eyes of the law and the people around them, but he knew they were already bound, as if they'd been destined for one another and maybe lived out this connection before. Because a love this big, a romance this earth-shattering couldn't be satisfied with just one lifetime.

Death do us part seemed too short a time to pledge his love, but he didn't want to go off script.

Frazer handed him the rings, and his hands shook when he placed one on Mallory's finger and she on his. Wedded for life. Bound for eternity.

He leaned down and captured her mouth with his.

"I'll never leave you again," he whispered in her ear.

She smiled into his eyes. "Yes, you will. But as long as we both come back to one another, that's all that matters."

CHAPTER TWENTY-FIVE

T HE AIR FELT cooler here after being in the south of France for a week, but smelled so sweetly of spring, so perfectly of home that Reilly preferred it a thousand times over to the dry, arid heat of the Mediterranean.

They'd broken a few of the laws of physics to get here, but they could relax now. The sun shone brightly and birds sang gaily as if celebrating with the happy couple. It wasn't like him to get all hearts and roses, but apparently, after thirty-eight years on this earth, it was finally his turn.

Izzy Campbell had provided a pale-blue, knee-length dress, white cardigan and sandals for Jane to wear, and a floral dress with a pretty headband for Taylor. Everything fit perfectly, even the shoes. Reilly could barely keep his eyes off the woman at his side, but forced himself to stop staring.

He faced forward.

The bride looked beautiful, elegant and regal. Alex looked stunned.

Reilly knew how the guy felt. He glanced at Jane again. He knew *exactly* how Alex felt.

It was probably dumb to fall so hard and fast, but he hadn't had much choice in the matter. The more time he'd spent with Jane the more time he'd wanted to spend with her. There'd been no way he was abandoning her on that boat.

Anthrax or no damn anthrax.

Her fingers rested on his thigh, and he took her hand in his. Even here, surrounded by hundreds of people, his body reacted to her presence.

They hadn't been alone much over the last few days, and Reilly hadn't even kissed her yet. The timing had been wrong. The place had been wrong.

She glanced over at him and blushed prettily when she caught him staring. He grinned. At least this attraction wasn't all one sided. But he wanted more than a physical relationship. More than a hard fuck against the nearest wall—although that would be good, too.

He rubbed his thumb over the smooth skin of the back of her hand as Alex and Mallory exchanged promises to love and honor one another. They skipped the "obey" part of the vows.

Spoilsports.

Taylor was watching the proceedings with awe. Reilly leaned toward Jane and waited for her to turn to face him, a question in her eyes. He slowly lowered his head and watched her breath hitch before she opened her mouth slightly. He took it as an invitation and pressed a gentle kiss on her lips, tasting what she offered. Then he pulled away and leaned back to watch the rest of the ceremony, clasping her hand tightly in his.

He needed to be careful not to freak her out after her last awful experience with love, but Reilly knew this was the real thing. Something that would last. Something that would grow into a shared home and shared family. He wouldn't rush it, in fact he was going to do his damnedest to court Jane the old-fashioned way for as long as his weak body could hold out.

She leaned up to whisper in his ear. "Am I still your client?"

Reilly shook his head.

"And do you consider me in a suitable mental place to decide who to have sex with?" she asked very quietly.

He gritted his teeth against the vision her words created. "Yes."

"Then I suggest you lock your door tonight unless you want a midnight visitor."

His mouth went dry. "Taylor—"

"Will be fine in the room next door."

Christ. He looked at Jane's sweetly determined expression, and his inner resolve cracked wide open. "I'll give you a key."

"Thank God."

"Amen."

CHAPTER TWENTY-SIX

FRAZER FINGERED THE small, white card with Izzy's name on it. He'd written it while sweating it out on that boat in the Med, waiting to see whether or not Alex had been exposed to anthrax and was in danger of imminent death. He'd added a small love heart to Izzy's name. She hadn't noticed that she was the only one with that love heart. He hadn't told her he'd been the one to painstakingly write half the cards at the reception.

He sipped on a glass of very expensive single malt Art Hanrahan had bought for him, a peace offering of sorts, while watching Alex and Mallory step up to get ready for their first dance as man and wife.

Izzy came up behind him, laced her fingers with his, and pulled him to his feet.

"Oh, no," he said, realizing what was happening.

"Yes." She said it sweetly, but there was no denying that hint of former Army captain in her tone. "It's your last official duty."

"Kit, save me," he pleaded with Izzy's little sister who sat at the table checking her phone.

"You're on your own, pal. But if you suck I will publicly disown you."

Frazer groaned as Izzy towed him to where Ashley Chen

and Lucas Randall stood beside the dance floor. Lucas gave him a look.

Frazer gave him one back. He pulled Izzy close. "Wait here for me. If I have to suffer I'm taking you with me."

She laughed up at him and he found himself captivated all over again by those green eyes and that elusive beauty mark near her mouth. "I thought you didn't dance, ASAC Frazer."

"I never said I didn't dance. I just said I don't like dancing."

"Ah, a subtle difference." She went to pull away.

"Wait for me," he insisted.

The music started, Nina Simone's "Feeling Good." He held out his hand to Ashley Chen who took it graciously. Alex and Mallory began dancing and everyone clapped and cheered. Frazer had to remind himself not to start weeping.

When Alex told Frazer he thought he'd been exposed to a new strain of anthrax, Frazer's insides had shattered. For a man who rarely let anyone close, Alex Parker had snuck under his guard remarkably quickly. Mallory, too. The idea of having to tell her Alex wasn't coming home…best not to think about it.

He twirled Ashley onto the dance floor, and into his arms. He knew the moves thanks to his expensive private schooling, and Ashley obviously knew the steps, too.

She was a remarkable human being. Sure, she was a little cool and aloof, he didn't generally trust people who weren't, but Ashley's survival story was inspiring.

Thankfully the song was a short one, and they escaped after only a minute or so. He bowed over Ashley's hand before leading her back to Lucas, who'd been dancing with Haley Cramer.

"Nice dancing with you, Ashley."

"You, too, boss."

"You can call me Lincoln when we're out of the office."

The agent smiled in surprise. She was regaining her confidence after her secrets had been brutally revealed. He wasn't one to let people off lightly. No point.

He spotted Izzy standing in the background. She didn't enjoy the spotlight and that suited him fine. He indicated she come over with a curl of his finger. She raised her brow but strolled toward him. She wore a champagne colored gown that fit her body like a glove. He slid his hand over the slippery fabric and pulled her close.

She skimmed her hands up to his shoulders. "You're actually a very good dancer."

He smiled at her. "You sound surprised."

"Nothing about you surprises me anymore." She laughed.

He spun them around the dance floor and saw Kit cringe in the background. He winked at Kit and then kissed Izzy on the lips, showing her just how much he'd missed her this week. Izzy grinned when he let her come up for breath.

"I'm very good at a lot of things," he said smugly.

"You know we have a room, right?"

"Kit has one, too, right?"

Izzy licked her lips, and he watched, riveted. "Adjoining. She's sharing with Becca."

Frazer nodded. "Thank God. As long as we can lock the door."

"You have something in mind?" Izzy asked, not so innocently.

"I have plenty in mind, Dr. Campbell."

"Maybe we should run up and make sure we have everything we need for the night?" Izzy suggested, moving even closer.

"You don't think I'll be missed?" asked Frazer, taking a quick look around, torn between duty and desire.

"We'll be quick." She leaned up and nibbled his ear lobe. "And Barney and Rex are in our rooms. I should make sure they're okay."

He pulled away and looked down at her. "And now, come to think of it, there was one thing I wanted to get from my bag. A wedding present."

"I thought we'd already given the happy couple a gift?"

"We did, but I managed to get them something else that will make them both very happy."

"What is it?" Her eyes glinted with curiosity.

"A job offer." At her confused look he added, "I put Moira Henderson's name forward for a position at headquarters. Gave her a glowing recommendation."

"She got the job?"

Frazer felt his grin spread. "Starts in two weeks. Mallory might not get the chance to even say goodbye to the woman."

Izzy laughed "And this is a good thing?"

He nodded.

"Well, we're going to need that letter and to check on the dogs. Assuming you want me to come with you?" Izzy asked innocently.

Frazer nodded. "I'm going to need help carrying everything."

Izzy laughed and led him off the dance floor.

CHAPTER TWENTY-SEVEN

"WHERE DO YOU think they're going?" Mallory asked Alex, eyeing Lincoln and Izzy heading out of the reception as furtive as thieves.

"Exactly where I'd be going if I didn't have two hundred people watching my every move," Alex said, tightening his grip on the spot where her waist used to be.

She chuckled, leaning her head against his shoulder. "That's what got us into this situation in the first place."

He kissed her forehead. "Me being a lucky bastard is what got us into this situation."

"You weren't so lucky this week, were you?" Mallory said softly. He hadn't told her what had happened, but she knew it wasn't good.

He shook his head. "I'll tell you about it tomorrow."

Jane Sanders was dancing nearby with Jack Reilly, who sent Mallory a wink. They were both keeping a close eye on a little, blonde girl who was jumping up and down nearby with Michael Vincent, Vivi's son, who was giggling audibly.

The boy was talking now, a miracle of circumstance and the right kind of therapy. The general consensus was he was on the edge of the autism spectrum, but he'd been selectively mute as a result of a traumatic childhood experience. He was making good progress in a new school.

"Did you almost die?" she asked Alex quietly, dreading the answer.

His fingers flexed, pulling her closer. "Not exactly. But for a little while I thought I might."

Tears gathered, but she blinked them away. "I'm very grateful you didn't."

He rubbed his palm up and down her back, soothing her. "Me, too."

"I thought we promised no more secrets?"

"We agreed no more lies. I didn't lie to you, Mal. You have my word. I was worried what the stress would do to you and the baby."

She met his troubled gaze with a wry look. "Don't do it again."

"No, ma'am, Mrs. Parker."

She felt her lip curl though she tried to quash it. "And now I'm afraid I'm going to lose you again."

He opened his mouth as if to argue but then must have spotted what she'd already seen—her mother approaching them with a purposeful gleam in her eye. He swore as he caught on to Mallory's meaning. Alex's new mother-in-law was claiming a dance.

Suddenly chaos erupted from near the entrance of the reception room and Mallory saw two fur balls, one black, one golden, race across the hardwood floor, jointly holding a stick, and inadvertently sending several people flying. Ouch. Half the room reached for their weapons before they realized it was just two harmless, if crazy, retrievers.

"How'd they get out?" Mallory wondered. Rex had been bunking with Barney for company. The main worry was the children becoming scared or getting knocked over. Alex stood in front of her while Reilly shepherded Michael and Jane's daughter, Taylor, off to one side.

Alex whistled to Rex, but both dogs had the bit between their teeth and were ready to run until they dropped. Mallory walked swiftly to the French doors off to the side at the back of the reception hall. She indicated the security guard open up and he obliged, throwing the doors wide. A split-second before the dogs headed toward freedom, she realized the cake was in the direct line of their escape.

Her mouth dropped, and she watched in alarm as the dogs ran full tilt toward it. Darsh Singh reached over and lifted the stand that the cake was set on a fraction of a second before the table beneath it was demolished.

The music stopped, and Mallory found herself staring in horrified anticipation at her mother who'd wanted and needed everything to be perfect.

Margret Tremont clapped her hands over her mouth and Mallory thought it was all over. And then the senator started laughing, and the whole room seemed to exhale a sigh of relief.

Security closed both sets of doors into the reception area in case the dogs decided to do a celebratory loop. Darsh laid the cake carefully on the nearest table and gave a mock bow.

Mallory started clapping, and Alex joined her with a sharp wolf whistle.

"Let's get that sucker cut before anything else can happen," Alex urged.

"What about the dogs?"

"We'll save them a piece." Alex then showed her his cell phone. A text from Frazer apologizing for letting the dogs out and telling him to be on the lookout for the mutts.

"Frazer can trudge through the fields after the dogs. You

and I are going to cut the cake, and then we're going to dance with your parents and each other for as long as you want. And, when you're done, or you need a break from all these people, I'm going to carry you up to our room and make love to you for hours."

"Carry me?" she said dubiously. She was no lightweight.

"Carry you," Alex insisted. He stepped closer. "And you're going to let me because I love you and I promised, in front of all these people, to worship you with my body. I hope to get started on that sooner rather than later."

Her heart went all fluttery. "Okay."

"Okay?" He gave her a stern look.

She just smiled at him. People said your wedding day was supposed to be the best day of your life, but she suspected there would be many, many more days to choose from and she intended to enjoy every one of them.

"I love you, Alex," she said tenderly.

"I love you, too, Mrs. Parker."

A COLD DARK PLACE

Cold Justice Series Book 1

Justice isn't always black or white.

Former CIA assassin Alex Parker works for The Gateway Project, a clandestine government organization hell-bent on taking out serial killers and pedophiles before they enter the justice system. Alex doesn't enjoy killing, but he's damn good at it. He's good at dodging the law, too—until a beautiful rookie agent has him wondering what it might be like to get caught.

FBI Special Agent Mallory Rooney has spent years hunting the lowlife who abducted her identical twin sister eighteen years ago. Now, during an on-going serial killer investigation, Mallory begins to suspect there's a vigilante operating outside the law. She has no choice but to take him down, because murder isn't justice. Is it?

Sometimes it's cold and dark.

When Mallory starts asking questions, The Gateway Project management starts to sweat, and orders Alex to watch her. As soon as they meet, the two begin to fall in love. But the lies and betrayals that define Alex's life threaten to destroy them both—especially when the man who stole her sister all those years ago makes Mallory his next target, and Alex must reveal his true identity to save the woman he loves.

COLD PURSUIT

Cold Justice Series Book 2

Single mom Vivi Vincent is thrust into her worst nightmare when she's trapped inside a mall during a terror attack along with her eight-year-old son. With the help of Jed Brennan, an FBI special agent on enforced leave, Vivi and her son survive the assault. But the danger is far from over.

Vivi's son may have witnessed critical details of the terrorists' future plans and is targeted for death, but he's mute, and he's traumatized. Still someone launches a strike against the FBI's safe house, and Jed fears the bad guys have an inside man. No longer knowing who to trust, he hides mother and son in a log cabin deep in the heart of the Wisconsin Northwoods. There Jed and Vivi try to figure out how to unlock the information inside her son's head. What they don't bargain for is the red-hot attraction that flares between them, or the extent of the sinister plot that threatens to rip apart not only any chance of happiness they might have together, but also the very fabric of American society.

COLD LIGHT OF DAY

Cold Justice Series Book 3

Physicist Scarlett Stone is the daughter of the man considered to be the most notorious Russian agent in FBI history. With her father dying in prison she's determined to prove he's innocent, but time is running out. Using a false identity, she gains access to the Russian ambassador's Christmas party, searching for evidence of a set-up.

Former Navy SEAL, now FBI Special Agent, Matt Lazlo, is instantly attracted to Scarlett but life is too complicated to pursue a politician's daughter. When he discovers she lied to him about her identity, he hunts her down with the ruthless efficiency he usually reserves for serial killers.

Not only does Scarlett's scheme fail, it puts her in the sights of powerful people who reward unwanted curiosity with brutality. The FBI—and Matt—aren't thrilled with her, either. But as agents involved in her father's investigation start dying, and the attempts to stop Scarlett intensify, Matt and his colleagues begin to wonder. Could they have a traitor in their midst?

As Scarlett and Matt dig for the truth they begin to fall passionately for one another. But the real spy isn't about to let anyone uncover their secrets, and resolves to remain firmly in the shadows—and for that to happen, Matt and Scarlett have to die.

COLD FEAR

Cold Justice Series Book 4

When old evidence turns up on a fresh corpse, ASAC Lincoln Frazer is determined it won't delay the execution of a convicted serial killer. But when more young women are brutally slain, it becomes clear—this new killer is intimately familiar with the old murders.

Former Army Captain Dr. Isadora Campbell helped her mother conceal a terrible crime. After her mother's death, Izzy resigned her commission and returned to the Outer Banks to raise her rebellious teenage sister. But it doesn't take long for Izzy to suspect that someone knows exactly what she did, all those years ago.

With pressure mounting to reopen the old case, Frazer will use any means possible to catch the killer. Thrust together during the investigation, he and Izzy find themselves reluctantly attracted to one another, and begin an affair. Meanwhile the killer is much closer than they think. Izzy's confession of her secret drives Frazer away as he struggles with her deception. By the time he realizes he's fallen in love with the stubborn woman, the killer has her. Now the race is on to save Izzy, and any chance of a future they might have together.

COLD IN THE SHADOWS

Cold Justice Series Book 5

CIA Officer Patrick Killion is on a secret mission to hunt down the ruthless female assassin hired to kill the Vice President of the United States. The trail leads him to the Colombian rainforest and an earnest biologist, Audrey Lockhart, whose work on poison dart frogs gives her access to one of the deadliest substances on earth—the same substance used to murder the VP.

When Audrey is attacked by the local drug cartel, Killion steps in and hustles her out of harm's way, determined to find out what she knows. His interrogation skills falter somewhere between saving her life and nursing her back to health as he realizes she's innocent, and he ends up falling for her. Audrey has a hard time overlooking the fact that Killion kidnapped her, but if she wants to get her life back and track down the bad guys, she has to trust him. Then someone changes the rules of their cat and mouse game and now they're the ones being hunted—by a cold-blooded killer who is much closer than they think.

COLD HEARTED

Cold Justice Series Book 6

Hunting For A Killer...

Detective Erin Donovan expects life to quiet down after the arrest and conviction of a serial rapist who terrified her university town last summer. Then two young women are brutally slain and the murders bear all the hallmarks of the campus rapist. Did Erin arrest an innocent man? Now her job is at stake and tensions are high and just when it looks like things can't get worse, her department gets the help it needs to solve the double homicide—in the form of a man Erin has never been able to forget.

Who Doesn't Play By The Rules.

FBI Agent Darsh Singh has no interest in reliving the past. Three years ago, his feelings for Erin Donovan had him breaking all his rules about getting involved. Now his only interest in the former NYPD detective is figuring out if she screwed up a rape investigation and helped send an innocent man to prison. But being forced to work together rekindles their old attraction, and as Darsh and Erin fall for each other, the campus predator fixates on Erin. The race is on to identify the ruthless killer before he makes Erin his final victim.

COLD SECRETS

Cold Justice Series Book 7

When an international ring of sex traffickers kidnaps an eight-year-old girl in Boston, FBI Agent Lucas Randall heads undercover. But his rescue operation goes disastrously wrong and Lucas barely escapes with his life. Now the ruthless traffickers are hunting him down, along with everyone else who threatens their operation.

Computer expert Ashley Chen joined the FBI to fight against evil in the world—evil she experienced firsthand. She has mad skills, and deadly secrets, and once she starts working with Lucas, she also has big trouble, because after years of pushing people away, she's falling for the guy. The feeling is more than mutual, but as Ashley intensifies her online pursuit of the trafficking ring, her traumatic past collides with her present and suddenly Lucas can't tell which side she's on. And as the case escalates into a high-stakes game of cat and mouse, it turns out Ashley isn't the only one with something to hide.

If neither can trust the other with their secrets, how can they trust each other with their hearts?

COLD MALICE

Cold Justice Series Book 9

ASAC Steve (Mac) McKenzie is out to prove himself by leading a task force investigating a series of murders in the heart of Washington, DC. His undercover work in an antigovernment compound twenty years earlier is related—as is the sweet, innocent girl he befriended back then. Now that girl is a beautiful woman, and she has something to hide.

Tess Fallon spent a lifetime trying to outrun her family's brand of bigotry, but someone is threatening her anonymity by using the anniversary of her father's death to carry out evil crimes and she's terrified her younger brother is involved. She sets out to find the truth and comes face-to-face with a man she once idolized, a man she thought long dead. As the crimes escalate it becomes obvious the killer has an agenda, and Tess and Mac are running out of time to stop him.

Will the perpetrator use a decades-old dream of revolution to attack the federal government? And will the fact that Tess and Mac have fallen hard for each other give a cold-hearted killer the power to destroy them both?

COLD JUSTICE SERIES OVERVIEW

A Cold Dark Place (Book #1)
Cold Pursuit (Book #2)
Cold Light of Day (Book #3)
Cold Fear (Book #4)
Cold In The Shadows (Book #5)
Cold Hearted (Book #6)
Cold Secrets (Book #7)
Cold Malice (Book #8)
A Cold Dark Promise (Book #9~A Wedding Novella)

Watch out for Book #10 in 2018!

Cold Justice Series books are also available as audiobooks
narrated by Eric Dove. See Toni's website for details
(www.toniandersonauthor.com)

ACKNOWLEDGMENTS

In August this year, I attended a writing retreat in the lovely town of Shawano, Wisconsin (not far from where I set *Cold Pursuit*) with four of the most talented and wonderful people I know (Kathy Altman, Jenn Stark, Carolyn Crane and Rachel Grant). It was a time of furious plotting and artistic rejuvenation. Before I went to Wisconsin I'd realized there was something missing from this novella and they helped me figure out what that something was. Needless to say, this was a lot of story to try and fit into a forty-thousand-word format, but I hope you enjoy the results of my labors. I wanted Alex and Mallory to have the best wedding possible, considering all the pain their journey has involved. But there was no way I could write more than a chapter or two about an actual wedding. I'd always intended to reveal more of Jane Sanders's tragic past and this was the perfect opportunity. Despite what some reviewers will undoubtedly say, this is not the last *Cold Justice Series* book, although I am contemplating a possible spin-off at some point.

Thanks, as always, to Kathy Altman for being my critique partner. She breaks down my stories and seems to understand my brain (no mean feat). And thanks to Rachel Grant for the beta read despite her busy schedule.

Thanks to my editors, Alicia Dean, and Joan Turner at JRT Editing, for the polish (commas are my kryptonite). My cover artist, Syd Gill, who, as always, did a great job capturing the essence of the story in pictorial form. And Paul Salvette (BB eBooks) who formats my ebooks with such care, and the guys at Createspace who take care of the print book interiors.

I'm pretty sure I've forgotten someone, maybe Martha Stewart for her "*Weddings*" magazine or Pinterest for feeding me everything else I needed to visualize the wedding, plot and characters.

As always, I want to thank my husband for being awesome, and my kids for being the best people in the world (and, yes, I'm biased!).

DEAR READER

Thank you for reading *A Cold Dark Promise*. I hope you enjoyed Alex and Mallory's wedding story. Please note, this is *not* the last book in the *Cold Justice Series*. Expect more next year.

1. If you have time, please help other readers find this book by writing a review. Thank you!

2. Sign up for my Newsletter (www.toniandersonauthor.com/newsletter) on my website to hear about new releases, special offers, and receive a FREE EBOOK!

3. Check out my website for exclusive short stories and extra content.

4. Interested in a writer's life? Come chat with me on Facebook (www.facebook.com/toniandersonauthor), follow me on Twitter (@toniannanderson), or check out some of my visual inspiration on Pinterest (www.pinterest.com/toniannanderson/).

Look out for book #10 in 2018!

ABOUT THE AUTHOR

New York Times and *USA Today* international bestselling author, Toni Anderson, writes dark, gritty Romantic Suspense novels that have hit #1 in Barnes & Noble's Nook store, Top 10 in the Amazon, iBooks, and Kobo stores. Her novels have won many awards, and she's been nominated for the prestigious Romance Writers of America® RITA® Award.

A former Marine Biologist from Britain, she inexplicably ended up in the geographical center of North America, about as far from the ocean as it is possible to get. She now lives in the Canadian prairies with her Irish husband and two children and spends most of her time complaining about the weather.

Toni has no explanation for her oft-times dark imagination, and only hopes the romance makes up for it. She's addicted to reading, dogs, tea, and chocolate.

If you want to know when Toni's next book will be out, visit her website (www.toniandersonauthor.com) and sign up for her newsletter. If you want to read other fascinating stories about life in a city that during winter is sometimes colder than Mars, friend her on Facebook: (www.facebook.com/toniannanderson).

Toni donates 15% of her royalties from EDGE OF SURVIVAL to diabetes research—to find out why, read the book!

Printed in Great Britain
by Amazon